"An enchanting and poignantly subtle story told with deft humor and thoughtful absences, where the initiation into mysteries is both esoteric and deeply personal."
—Caitlin Starling, author of *The Death of Jane Lawrence*

"Somehow both quiet and lively, both dreamlike and rock-solid, this magical novella feels like a story dropped in your ear at a party by a brand new friend."
—Freya Marske, author of *A Marvellous Light*

"By turns dazzling, profound, and tender, *Uncommon Charm* is intensely readable—I'd let this narrator regale me with anything that crossed her mind for hours on end. While her wit lights the room, her insights illuminate those around her. This story's rumination on magic, power, and human nature will stick with me for years to come."
—Emma Mieko Candon, author of *The Archive Undying*

"A sparkling gem of a story, treading lightly but surely over subject matter both delightful and profound."
—Lara Elena Donnelly, author of *Base Notes*

"Chaotic magic mixes with the decadence of Russian aristocracy in this sparkling tale. While there are darker depths beneath its facets, a witty narrator and a host of drawing room adventures give this a brilliance and verve that will brighten your heart and keep you turning pages through to the very end. The best way to describe it? Charming. Utterly charming!"
—Wendy N. Wagner, author of *The Secret Skin*

Neon Hemlock Press
www.neonhemlock.com
@neonhemlock

Uncommon Charm
Emily Bergslien and Kat Weaver

Cover Illustration by Marlowe Lune
Cover Design by dave ring
Interior Illustration by Matthew Spencer

Print ISBN-13: 978-1-952086-38-0
Ebook ISBN-13: 978-1-952086-39-7

Emily Bergslien and Kat Weaver
UNCOMMON CHARM

Neon Hemlock Press

THE 2022 NEON HEMLOCK NOVELLA SERIES

Uncommon Charm

BY EMILY BERGSLIEN
AND KAT WEAVER

For Annie, Dena, Lara, Meagan, Sara, and true friends everywhere: you are magic.

"*There are few, indeed, who wish to penetrate into other spheres, higher or lower, in ways allowed or forbidden. Men, in the mass, are amply content with life as they find it. Therefore there are few saints, and sinners (in the proper sense) are fewer still, and men of genius, who partake sometimes of each character, are rare also.*

Yes; on the whole, it is, perhaps, harder to be a great sinner than a great saint."

Arthur Machen, The White People

London, 1925

ONE

THREE DAYS after I was expelled from the Marable
School for Girls, our poor Simon arrived. My mother
told me to expect him, so when the bell rang, I
opened the door onto a gloomy November sky, a gloomy
November street, and a gloomy November of a boy. (And
boy he was, only twenty years old to my sixteen.) He was
short and nicely strong, wiry, with tanned cheeks and big
dark eyes. Not at all like his father—but on second glance,
there did lurk a spectre of Uncle Vee in his prettyish face,
down which a raindrop gently rolled. He'd already doffed
his hat; those slick curls of his would be ruined.

"You're Mr. Wolf," I said. "Or is it Mr. Koldunov now?"

The car behind him hadn't left yet. I saluted the
Koldunovs' driver, Tom, to let him know everything was
well, he'd safely delivered the goods, he needn't subject
himself to the weather. Simon and I could surely handle
his single, very sad suitcase. Tom returned my wave and
drove away.

"Er," said our guest. "Mr. Wolf will do. You're Miss Selwyn-Stirling?"

"When I care to answer to it, but don't call me *miss* around the Koldunovs. They'll tease you, and not in the nice you're-one-of-us-now way."

"Thanks for the advice," he said, and he continued to stand on our doorstep, looking about and letting himself be drizzled upon. I wondered why until I realised, oh no, he was waiting for me to invite him inside, at which point I decided I would walk to the moon and back for my new friend.

Grandly, I bowed him into the front hall. As he was taking off his wet things—he clutched his coat and hat until I nodded at the rack, strange boy, it was *right there*—Muv appeared on the first floor landing, at the top of the stairs.

You'd have thought Simon was a bird that'd biffed itself against a window instead of a student meeting his new mentor, though he wasn't wrong to find Muv intimidating. From his point of view, I'd have seen not only a small, brisk woman whose bobbed auburn hair absolutely guillotined her jaw, whose freckles foxed her face like that rust on old books, whose black suit cut her body into clean ink lines, but the most ruthless magician England had ever borne. And she was a pretty ruthless mother, too.

"Good afternoon, Mr. Wolf," she said. "You may address me as Lady Aloysia, my lady, or ma'am." It was her way of trying to set him at ease, laying out the protocol, only she was always so dreadfully blunt about answering questions you hadn't asked. More embarrassing still, Simon's nod became a strange half-bow.

"Oh, don't," I groaned.

"Julia will show you around the house." Muv fixed an eye on me. "His room first, please. You will not make him haul his luggage everywhere. Is there more?"

Simon's hands tightened around the handle. "No, ma'am. Just the one."

"Very well. We will meet for dinner three hours from now. Do tell me whether I've correctly understood your dietary needs."

"Muv, honestly, you needn't be the lepidopterist pinning butterflies. You can ask him these things like you're both human people."

She gestured for me to take the suitcase. I hefted it before Simon could object.

"I—thanks, Miss Sel—er, Lady Aloysia, ma'am, no, it's—" Simon grasped uselessly at the air. "Thanks, but you don't have to do all that."

Muv tapped her elbow. "I see. Julia, after you help Mr. Wolf get settled, please inform Beth the week's menu may remain as it is. I asked," she continued, both addressing him and chiding me, "because I would not put it past Madam Koldunova to serve you roast pork every day."

"It was every other day," said Simon.

Muv blinked down at him. He blinked up at her. Silence could be loud indeed. An entire three-second opera played out as I started to drag the suitcase upstairs.

Simon's footsteps came in a flurry after me, and, generous girl that I was, I let him take charge of his own belongings. When we reached the second floor, he turned back with a perplexed look, but Muv had disappeared into her laboratory. He couldn't have expected hugs and smiles, not from the Lady Aloysia Stirling, not with her reputation, though I knew for a fact he'd received colder welcomes: I had the whole of it from Marie and Adele Koldunova. After three weeks with the Koldunovs, Muv ought to seem downright tropical.

"Er," Simon murmured, "did you see—?" Though I tilted my head, yes, do go on, he shuttered himself. "Never mind."

"These games are unnecessary, you know. You don't have to keep secrets, and you don't have to doubt your eyes. I can help! I did grow up here. Muv never fails to keep a thread in her needle, not that I pay her magic any mind.

It is *so* tedious when your mother always knows where you are and what you're thinking, but you'll find out soon enough. I didn't see anything. What did you see?"

"A woman," Simon said, startled into answering. "Not your mother, but tall and blonde. A bit, er, bony. And bleeding."

"Oh, well. I should have expected you'd be a medium. Come along!" I bounded up the stairs. "The ghosts will wait."

TWO

$\int$IMON'S BEDROOM was on the second floor, down the hall
from mine. I had the street view; he had the back garden
and the former coach house, which now accommodated
both Grandad's London car and its driver, Bill. After I
showed Simon the washroom and all that, the right way to
pull the lavatory chain so the bowl wouldn't overflow, my
duckling toddled after me into the library. Though it was
neither large nor equipped with books of interest to the
modern reader, the itch in his fingers was unmistakable.

"Ha," I said, "I knew you'd venerate the written word,
you're just the sort. The novels in my room are better.
Borrow anything you like from there or here, only mind
the spiders, they skulk about these high ceilings especially.
It's hard to keep up the place, you know. Grandad can't
spare us more than Dolly and Beth, and Muv's too
particular to bring on anyone else."

When I'd mentioned spiders, Simon looked up as
though he expected a plump specimen to descend upon
his nose. I had to laugh.

As we left the library for the main staircase, I did him the favour of explaining Muv. It was only right to let him know what to expect. "She's a very private person, Muv is, even magicked herself out of needing a lady's maid— someone to remind her when to eat and sleep and get out of bed, like she had when I was very young. She's always had a mania for her work, I swear, she wouldn't have fun at all if it weren't for Uncle Vee."

Simon used his ongoing search for spiders as an excuse not to talk. I didn't mind. He needed time for his new circumstances to sink in.

"Don't tell her I told you all this, though she'll pluck it from your head anyhow." I gave him a nudge. "Next time she has her gloves off, you'll notice the scars. Oh! Do let's say hullo to the sheep."

I made Simon pause with me before the paintings along the stair: the bucolic landscapes and the portraits of Muv's relations, the stuffy art she could neither replace nor sell, nor, if it were up to her, burn on the street. The house wasn't hers and never would be. My grandfather, the Earl of Barrowbeck, was letting us live here until he died. Not only would I inherit the house, I'd get everything else he would have left to her. He'd cut Muv out of the will when she got divorced.

"She and my father split after the war," I continued. "Before I was born, they lived in all sorts of places, Paris and Vienna and Hong Kong, but she made him leave London when I was nine. I don't know the old pater well, he's rich and a Tory, and worst of all a terrible bore. Now he's in Germany with his pack of wolfhounds and his priceless medieval tapestries."

Simon thrust his hands in his pockets as we progressed up the stairs.

"I am led to believe a great many things happened to my mother," I said. "Some of them weren't even her fault. Watch your step! That floorboard creaks, no good for midnight sneaking."

We strolled through the nursery, its sparse furniture draped in sheets.

We paused in every drawing room so I could point out how each one was more Victorian and unnecessary than the last.

We went down to the kitchen, where I introduced Simon to Dolly and Beth before passing along Muv's message about the menu. He cleared his throat and murmured something about not wanting to be a bother.

We traversed the dining room, its curtains closed over the rain. I rightly informed Simon that the burgundy velvet and oak panels would stifle us to death if we stayed too long. With shy humour he replied that after an excruciating dinner, death might be a relief, to which I agreed, but dinners were always fun when they included me. I swept my fingers down the long table for the pleasure of its slick surface and detached myself with a cheerful rap. Onward!

"I don't suppose you read *Tatler*? Neither do I, Muv doesn't subscribe, but I steal Marie and Adele's when I have the chance. I like the old issues, it's such fun digging up the dreadful things everyone's parents got up to, but they're terribly vague about how your father's brother died. I wish they'd kept more than the society journals. The inquest wasn't only gossip, it was news. What's the matter?"

We'd made our way to the outside of Muv's first floor laboratory, which was what everyone started calling the ballroom as soon as the wounded soldiers stopped coming. Though its big French window was overhung with drapes, it retained the once-famous electric chandeliers. We would not admire them today; I didn't have a key. I only supposed I'd ought to show him where he would be studying.

As I talked, he'd sunk to new depths of quietude. Perhaps he was nobly suffering the sight of another ghost, I thought, but after several seconds he said, "I have trouble thinking of him as my father."

"You and everybody else." Seeing his lip twist, I added, "Would you rather I lie?"

"Suppose not." He peeled himself from the wall. "Thanks for the tour."

"You're off to be alone in your room, aren't you? I'm sorry I didn't ask you anything about your life. I'd say I wanted to spare you from repeating yourself when Muv applies the thumbscrews this evening, but that would be a lie—I got carried away and forgot. Forgive me?" I furnished him with another brilliant smile. "You can tell me everything about yourself later, I promise."

Though his bloomed more hesitantly than mine, a smile was a smile. "Right," he said, "and you can tell me how you got expelled."

THREE

THOUGH Muv insisted we dress for dinner as a gesture of respect, it only made Simon feel more shabby and out-of-place. He still had on the afternoon's brown suit. "Don't worry," I said, "I didn't wave or even comb my hair, see?" I motioned at my fair, feathery cloud of a bob. "And Muv is wearing the same stockings."

She acknowledged me with a sigh and a stir of her soup.

"Oh, Muv, do you know any blonde women who died?"

Spoon nearly to his lips, Simon gazed in horror at Muv and me, especially Muv, but she only said, "Why do you ask?"

"Simon saw her earlier. He's a medium."

"Many magicians are," Muv replied. "Ghosts have never appeared for me, but Vladimir's sister, your aunt," nodding at Simon, "used to set out tea parties for them. Magic is a matter of leaving oneself open to experiences beyond the ordinary, and accepting the extraordinary in the everyday. As with every discipline, practice begets improvement."

"Do you know the blonde woman, though?"

"Yes," she said. "Mr. Wolf, would you care to ask me any questions about what you will be studying?"

"It was supposed to be just the two of you," I confided to him. "You're lucky I'm here to chaperone."

"Er," he said.

If I was being a pest, Muv deserved it for that comment about practice. I'd never practised at anything in my life. I never needed to. I would always be the cleverest cat in the room, which wasn't difficult when it was filled with peers and their spawn, but even if some lordly egg finally disgorged a genius, I wouldn't begrudge my defeat.

Muv sipped her claret, leaving me to deduce for myself why she hadn't risen to my bait. All right. It was my discomfiting Simon to which she objected. He kept raising and lowering his spoon without so much as a sup.

Sorry for his sake, almost, I said, "I'll not make another peep, I promise. Unless it is *very* funny."

"I'll laugh," Simon offered, and then, finally, as though bracing himself, he turned to Muv. "In your letter, ma'am, you mentioned something about making the magic you need. What does that mean if it was passed down from— er—?"

"Is that what Vladimir told you? And yet he would believe it. Allow me to correct his misconceptions."

"Of course, ma'am." He worried at the napkin on his lap. "I'm all ears for anything you've got."

With my half-glass of wine, I drank down facetious warnings: She'll experiment on you, Simon! She'll lock you in her laboratory and drain your blood into hundreds and hundreds of exquisitely-labelled vials! She'll catch you in a web of wards and haul dire secrets from your ensorcelled lips! Beware!

Muv wouldn't really do any of it but the last, and then only if he made her very angry indeed. Even I had never managed that.

I wondered what she thought of the anxieties that were doubtless knocking about Simon's skull, whether he was the right protégé for her, whether they would get on. Magician or not, I already liked having another person about the place.

I raised my eyebrows at him, you're in for it now, when Muv started her favourite lecture, the one in which she claimed anyone could enact magic, whether or not they regarded it as such, because magic could be anything. Why impose limits on the limitless? The persons most inclined towards magic were those whose experiences of reality were already at odds with the norm. If few of them actually made the leap and called themselves magicians, even fewer gained any sort of public acknowledgment for it. Muv would always insist her renown was due to her class.

My fork was more interesting than this old speech, but Simon hadn't heard it five thousand times. Though he mainly stared somewhere in the vicinity of Muv's plate, like a dainty fawn he occasionally ventured a beautiful brown-eyed glimpse above her head. So: whatever his feelings were about being a magician, about his magic not coming from Uncle Vee, curiosity *was* among them.

Staying with the Koldunov family was always the best part of my life, but the past three weeks couldn't have been nice for Simon. He was too, too common, Marie and Adele said, and I had believed them. What was Simon's opinion of the Koldunovs? They may have been my third cousins and my first friends, but—

Arthur was fundamentally incapable of understanding anything beyond rugby or rowing, despite his being at Oxford, and he was no ally for Simon besides. Marie and Adele were already each other's best friends, their conversation comprehensible only to us schoolgirls, even though they didn't attend school. The family had decided the fees were better spent on Joseph, who was collecting the prettiest boys at Eton. Georgia, the eldest, would rather contemplate her own perfection than give consequence to us lesser children, and Lizzie was six entirely useless years old. Their mother Dahlia was always kind to me, but I wasn't her husband's illegitimate Jewish son. And then there was Vladimir Nikolaevich himself, a grand prince of nowhere.

When I was thirteen, Uncle Vee put on a shadow play for us children in which the puppets danced before he moved his hands. When I was ten, he and Aunt Dahlia disappointed but did not surprise high society by attending a fancy dress party as the Marquis de Sade and Justine. When I was born, he deluged Muv with a room's worth of flowers, orchids and roses and irises, all of which she sent straight back to his door.

Muv was supposed to have married Uncle Vee. She'd been promised to his elder brother first, but she was only seventeen when Prince Nikolai Nikolaevich died, not quite old enough to be out in society. After Muv met my father and broke things off with Uncle Vee, he worked himself into a huff and eloped with pretty Miss Dahlia Winfield, his artist friends' favourite muse.

Luck all around, in my opinion. I got to be my own delightful self, and I got to have the Koldunovs as my friends. Poor Simon, surrounded by lovely un-princes and un-princesses, but not one of them would have discussed magic with him.

Thus his dismay when Muv said, "Magic defies explanation."

"I thought explanations were why I was here. Ma'am."

Since his obvious emotional turmoil prevented him from eating any pudding, I reached across the table. He bit back a smile and pushed the bowl at me.

"You are here," Muv said, "because Vladimir grew bored with you when you did not perform to the unreasonable and arbitrary standards he'd barely attempted to imagine. You and I, on the other hand, will explore philosophy.

We will find no answers, but we may learn how to ask questions."

What had Simon done to deserve such a fate? Winter was dreary enough without being forced to share a house with Muv.

"I have spent my life attempting to quantify intuition," she continued. "The work is often dull and unrewarding. I might go so far as to call it pointless, even paradoxical, but I persevere. Though I may not be able to explain magic, the rituals I develop help me to comprehend echoes of echoes. It is not dissimilar to studies which bring many people closer to their conceptions of the divine."

Another of those pauses ensued, during which Muv and Simon read entire books off of each other's faces.

"I understand," said Simon. "I'll give it a go."

"How long are you going to stay?" I asked, licking the last of the pudding from the back of my spoon. "Muv?"

Simon glanced at her, wondering the same thing.

Muv said, "As long as this partnership is worthwhile to him."

After dinner, I rescued Simon for myself. Given the choice between cards and chess, he picked cards, so we played rummy in the least overwrought of the drawing rooms. At school we would have made do with buttons, but here we found enough Dresden figurines to use as betting tokens. The shelves were better for our raid.

As I amassed a horde of my great-grandmother's ballet dancers and Marie Antoinettes, I set about my own interrogation.

"What's your mother like?"

"She's an artist. Draws cartoons, and she writes too, for the paper she and her friends put out. You'd call her a Bohemian."

"Which accounts for how you germinated," I said. "I suppose she was the one who contacted your father about your magic." Also, his bonny shepherdess was mine.

"She didn't like to do it."

"Then why did she?" I asked. "What happened?"
When he shrugged out of answering that one, I tried
another. "Did you always know who your father was, or
did she have to break the news?"

"You're cheating, and yes, I did."

"Did you ever think he'd acknowledge you?" I was most
certainly cheating. We were playing with my own deck,
which I'd been smart enough to mark when I was twelve.
See? I showed him the stars I'd needled onto the back
corner of every face card and ace. "Now we're even."

"Not quite. How'd you get yourself expelled?"

"A dare. I was caught with a flask of gin during maths."
A glib answer, but it wasn't a lie. "Numbers are so much
lovelier when *I* don't have to make them dance."

"Pedestrian, innit? I'd have pegged you for something
cleverer."

Flattered he'd let down his guard enough for that
breath of Hackney to slip out, I teased, "I've earned
your disapproval, Mr. Wolf! How long have we been
acquainted, five hours? For old folks like you, it usually
takes five minutes."

"I'll get the real story out of you, just you wait. And—
no," he said, fanning his cards face down. He became
very still and inward. I waited for the contemplative
breathing to finish, and my patience was rewarded: "I
thought me and him were happy to stay out of each
other's lives."

"If it weren't for the magic, he would have been."

"Right," said Simon, and the dear boy stared at the
table, desperately unable to say anything else, as though
I'd lent voice to his deepest, darkest musings instead of the
plain truth. This was not how his future was supposed to
have gone.

He picked up his cards.

When I glanced at my own hand, I noticed that the

top K on the king of spades was printed backwards. So
was the bottom letter and, yes, the king himself. How
funny, I thought. Then I realised that while I was still on
the sofa, I was seated on the opposite side of the table.
The fireplace was to my left instead of my right, and the
garden window had switched places with the portrait of
my great-grandmother. Though neither Simon nor I had
changed—the biggest freckle on my left arm remained in
place—the rest of the room had completely flipped.

"Sorry." Simon lowered his head into his hands.
"Sorry, sorry. I'll fix it."

"We're not trapped in a looking glass, are we?" I
opened the door into the hallway. The staircase seemed
normal, as processional as ever and persistently up-and-
down. No window had manifested on the wall, and the
big oval glass above the ormolu lamp failed to shine
with an unearthly light. "Good news!" I called over my
shoulder. "You only warped this room."

He groaned.

"I'd prefer a prettier renovation. Are we stuck with this
one?"

Simon's reply was muffled. "I hope not."

As a test, I brought one of the reversed playing cards
into the hall. The number three continued its masquerade
as a curvaceous E. When I tried the opposite, taking a
decorative plate from the hall into the room, its painted
landscape remained true to the artist's vision.

I'd reached the end of the easy logic, though I needn't
have bothered with this puzzle in the first place. It wasn't
mine to solve.

I laid down the plate beside Simon and his near-
corporeal anguish. "I'll get Muv, shall I? She'll want to
take notes."

We catalogued our observations until nearly two o'clock in the morning. Of course I was conscripted. Young ladies who wasted opportunities their mothers never had must perform their due penance. She never said as much, but I knew Muv. At least she rang for tea before Dolly went to sleep.

Not once did Simon complain, not when Muv sent him out to the garden so I could wave at him from beyond the looking glass, nor when she asked him to measure the room's dimensions with a knotted string, nor when she made him document everything we said before the switch. He lapped up the direction because for so long he'd lacked anything of the kind.

Muv saw it too. "This is false productivity," she warned. "We will not solve anything. We will happen upon no special clue. We are only tricking ourselves into thinking we have control, but the alternative is to sit here and sip our tea. Do you understand? We must either do everything we can, or do nothing at all."

I raised my hand. "Can I choose nothing?"

"No."

Simon's pen paused. "Well, ma'am, I—I've encountered similar ideas. Do what good you can in this world, right?"

"Faith can be essential to one's understanding of magic," Muv agreed, though to what I was not exactly certain. "Apart from formal religious practice, one might have one's own set of rituals." She laid her ungloved hands across the back of the sofa, beside Simon's shoulder. I jerked my head at him, look!—but he spared only a quick glance at the scars, pale remnants of the hundreds of scabs she'd picked at over the years. Instead, and with great intent, he met her eyes as she continued, "A sacrifice. A rhyme, a chant, a sigil. A balanced equation. Or not." She withdrew. "Continue your notes, Mr. Wolf. Take down whatever strikes you as necessary. The temperature, the barometric pressure, the time, your hand of cards.

I see you were not the winner."

"Yes, ma'am. Er. No, ma'am, I was not."

"So sorry," I said, settling into the armchair I'd commandeered.

"Julia, what are you doing with those books?"

"Looking, since you won't let me go to bed. *What* a mother. It's the wee hours of the morn, and you're here in your robe, haranguing strange men. To think of the example you're setting your only daughter!"

"You are writing. What about?"

The heft of my sigh would have moved mountains. "I'm underlining funny inverted words." I might construct a backwards cipher one day, though to what purpose, I didn't know. I hadn't any classes during which to pass notes. Coming up with the ciphers was always the best part, at any rate, never mind putting them to use.

"Do be careful," said Muv, "or you might find yourself enacting magic."

"Quelle horreur, how funny you are. If I copy out some examples, I can vouchsafe any spells or whatnot into your capable hands," I said, starting a new page. It was the best she'd get from her delinquent offspring.

Soon after I presented my list to her, she dismissed Simon and me.

He lingered in the doorway. "You're not coming, ma'am? Are you sure you don't need more help?"

"No, thank you; you've done enough work this evening." Muv brought down every lamp except the one nearest the sofa, where she took her seat. With the heavy silk of her robe draped down her arms and the soft light slanting across her face, she looked like another version of herself, someone who was almost kind. She tucked her hair behind her ear and bent over her journal. Her voice was hardly more than a murmur: "I'll finish the rest of it on my own."

I tugged Simon along. My eyeballs were about to drop

back into my throat, I was so tired, and while he gladly would have foregone sleep for the chance to see Muv work, I promised him other, better, more convenient opportunities would arise. This time she was going to stay awake until magic left the room.

It happened at five forty-three a.m., she informed us late the next morning. In case we were wondering.

FOUR

THERE WASN'T much about school I missed. Sport had been young Miss Julia's speciality, both curriculum-sanctioned and otherwise. I was friendly with all the girls because I made them laugh and never passed up a dare, but after Charlotte Henley and I were quits, I was the one who had to lubricate the social machinery, as it were.

We were sixth-formers now, Char had said, running her fingers through her newly-bobbed curls. Practice was all very well, but hadn't we ought to move on to the real thing? She hoped I hadn't taken our little get-togethers too seriously, and I hadn't, not a bit, but the way she said it brought out a spiteful determination to prove I could still be friends. Crossing swords with her hadn't been the same since.

At least I no longer had to trudge through what was supposed to be an education. I could read any detective novel I pleased, I could put on the wireless any time I liked, and, weather and mother permitting, perhaps I could even go out and admire shop displays with Marie and Adele.

Further on the positive side, the London house had
Simon; on the negative, Muv, but most importantly there
was no fencing club.

While Muv and Simon walked patterns into the streets,
or developed maps of the subconscious, or whispered the
names of angels at certain bricks, whatever dire nonsense
their studies led them to perpetrate, I performed my
foil drills up in the old nursery. My enthusiasm always
drained after ten minutes; I was bored without other girls
to trounce. When I asked Simon whether he would be a
proper necromancer and conjure a ghost for me to duel,
he gave real thought to the possibility before he caught on
and laughed.

All but the first week, when he'd been too shy to accept
Muv's offer, every Friday afternoon he would take a cab
back to the East End, and every Sunday he would return
in time for breakfast. He wasn't surprised we didn't attend
church. Muv had opinions, and I was lazy. Oh, but I did
miss sausage with our eggs. He should have known better
than to prevaricate about keeping kosher. Muv lived in the
truths people didn't tell.

After several more or less pleasant weeks living with
Simon, Uncle Vee invited us to lunch at the Ritz.

I wore my pearl earrings with my best cashmere
cardigan, and Muv settled on a chic russet suit from
Paris. Though Simon did have new clothes by then, his
being embarrassed was a fact not only of circumstance
but of life. Once we'd been in our chairs for a few
minutes, Muv made me switch places with him, so he
could have his back to the mirrored wall. Perhaps he was
too distracted by the sight of himself dining among *these*
people, in *this* fine restaurant, with the murals and the
marble and the bronze. He kept twisting his fingers as
though he had on invisible rings, and he refused to look
at the waiters. Muv and I hardly would have noticed
them otherwise.

Uncle Vee was late. At his entrance, finally, more than a few heads turned. Prince Vladimir Nikolaevich was both notorious and easily identified. He walked with a cane, not unusual nowadays, and while he did not discuss the truth of why he needed a wooden left foot, he'd given his children and me a great many stories on which to chew. The old injury only added to his charm; his beauty was famous enough, his youth immortalised in the world of art. At forty-something he was slightly faded, his curls none so black as they were, nor his features as cut-glass fine, and heavy pain lines marked his mouth and eyes— but oh, those eyes. They were like blue diamonds.

Though all of the Koldunov children were pretty, only Georgia could channel his particular glamour. I never doubted it was magic, how the two of them reeled the world to their will with nothing but a smile. It was terribly unfair.

"Alya, Alyechka," Uncle Vee said, kissing each of Muv's cheeks and taking her hands as she stood. She was more than a head shorter than he was. "You are radiant. You are perfect. Wear autumn always." He touched her lower lip.

"Volodya," she said.

Simon stared at the table.

Uncle Vee came to me next, clasping my hand and planting a solid kiss upon my forehead. "Little Peaseblossom! How *is* your proud Titania, my dear? You must tell me, she won't. I've not seen my fey girls for an age."

"I last dined with you on October the twenty-third," said Muv. "I am well, thank you for asking. Now sit." She indicated the empty place between her and Simon.

"You see, she is herself," I told Uncle Vee.

"No better a thing for your mother to be." Only when a waiter drew out his chair for him did Uncle Vee seem to notice Simon. "Well, boy. How's the magic, then?"

Simon came a beat late to the proffered handshake. "Still happening, sir?"

"He turned into a flock of starlings last week," I said. "One second he was showing me boxing manoeuvres, and the next—birds. We had to open the windows for them, they got so restless inside."

"I see. I *see*." He curled a finger on his lips. "And how did that feel?"

"Not like much of anything, sir," Simon answered. "It went right eventually."

"I did have to feed his arm for a few days while they caught up with the rest of him," I added. "I counted five starlings on my window sill, though one of them might have been wild."

"Ah," said Uncle Vee, "would that we all could so gracefully welcome an untamed creature into our hearts."

Muv tapped the table, unimpressed.

The waiter brought another round of beverages. Coffee for Uncle Vee, tea for Muv and me, and for Simon a deep draught of mineral water. His eyes were active, flashing from me to Muv and back again, and from Uncle Vee's face to somewhere over his shoulders on either side. I supposed that would be the ghosts. Anybody of a certain age, especially from our family, was bound to have them. I wondered whether a ghost or two hung over every shoulder at the Ritz, whether Simon was seeing them all, or whether some necessary emotional resonance meant he was only burdened with ours.

But magic, I told myself, wasn't my responsibility. I shouldn't think too hard.

Talk moved along. Uncle Vee asked me how many scoundrels I'd dueled of late, and our lunch arrived. Then he asked what egregious sin I had committed to get myself expelled from the Marriageable School for Girls, as he called it, and a waiter rescued Simon's dropped fork.

"Instead of an essay about Charlemagne, I wrote limericks comparing each of our mistresses to a different insect," I admitted, which was also true.

"What a pity they'd no appreciation of your talents." Once his coffee had been topped up, Uncle Vee opened a small cloisonné case and stirred in the drug of the hour. He sipped and sighed again, "What a pity! Georgie had such good things to say about her time there."

That was because Georgia was perfect. "I like to think I've left my mark. Simon, did you ever do anything ridiculous at school?"

"Not intentionally." His smile wobbled.

Though I tried to pull Simon into the conversation every chance I got, he resisted. If he'd only wanted to concentrate on being haunted, I'd have left him to his angst, but I couldn't let Uncle Vee forget his own son was right there. Uncle Vee didn't intend to ignore people, he never did. He just acted with the sincere belief that the most interesting person in his life was himself.

I sat with a sensation I'd otherwise experienced only on the rare occasions I was alone with Muv and Uncle Vee. When the two of them drew near each other, the rest of the world grew paler, myself included. The other Koldunovs solidified reality, reminded me I had a place as one beloved child among many. Now it was Simon and me, each of us the reflection of a parent to whom we could not possibly compare. I'd turned out badly, which was mostly my fault, but for Simon it was sheer rotten luck. He didn't choose to be the natural son of an exiled prince.

When Muv suggested Simon and I take a walk in the park nearby, we leaped to fetch our coats and scarves. Uncle Vee put on an exaggerated show of protest that no one believed. Muv was still his favourite. He'd never admit he wasn't hers.

Simon and I had the park nearly to ourselves. No snow covered the dry leaves; no sun cut through the clouds. Our breath came in huge, cold puffs.

"Your mother," he said, "is terrifying."

"More so than usual?" I invitingly replied.

"She was doing magic the entire time. Incredible. If she hadn't told me what to look for, I'd never have noticed."

"Oh—she told you."

"It's a lesson, right? She wanted me to watch her. To listen." He inhaled. "Prince Vladimir, she...I'm not sure how to put it. It's not that she had him on strings. The world just danced along her lines. Systems she's been making and using for years, like she'd spun hundreds of webs but only plucked the threads she needed today."

"Why, though? What was she doing?"

Simon stopped at the entrance to a tree-lined path. "I don't know. But think about it, Jules, remember. Any time he spoke to you, really, every time, one of the waiters came round for some reason or another."

Why me? "That *is* their job."

"It is! They weren't magicked into anything they wouldn't have done otherwise. The timing, though, the precision—"

I scooped his arm into mine and pulled him into a stroll. "I believe you. It's strange, that's all."

"The whole lunch was strange."

"Let's have the rest of it, then. Which ghosts were they?"

There had been two: a girl of about twelve, her long black hair in ringlets, her neck bent at a cruel angle; and a slim gentleman perhaps a few years older than Simon, bleeding from explosive wounds in his head and chest. While the girl had touched Muv's wrist and then vanished, the man had lingered, passing his hand along Uncle Vee's shoulders before he settled his fingers on Muv's neck, where the invisible blood left no stain, and bent for a kiss.

I wrinkled my nose. "Your aunt and uncle."

"Oh. Your mother mentioned her—but what happened?"

"Lizaveta Nikolaevna, that's who baby Lizzie is named for, she was Uncle Vee's younger sister. She fell down the stairs. Everyone is very careful to say it was an accident." My look told him what I thought of that excuse. "She was Muv's friend. I've seen pictures of them together, frilly in white with enormous sleeves and bows behind their necks. Her grave might be important to a ritual of Muv's, I'm not certain, but she visits on occasion, brings flowers and presses her pricked thumb to the stone and so on. No one pretends Lizaveta the First never existed. Nikolai Nikolaevich died later. 1900, so says his grave. Carved below his sister's."

Our shoes crunched over desiccated leaves.

"I hadn't realised she was dead," Simon said. "May her memory be a blessing?"

He felt something, clearly. Not for Nikolai or poor Liza themselves, but for the fact of having a family about whom he'd never once cared. Perhaps he was wondering whether he was supposed to care now, whether that was correct. After all, he'd been visited by their ghosts.

"The Koldunovs will act as though you already know these things," I said. "Muv too, often enough. As though the souls of the damned should have imparted their wisdom to you the moment you set foot on Koldunov ground. I say, there's a thought." I blew a cloudy breath into his face. "You can see ghosts, but can you talk to them? Have you ever tried?"

"I thought I shouldn't. Your body—"

"My body?"

"Jules!" He nudged me with his elbow. "A body dies, all right, but there's the soul. How do I explain this? The part inside that looks and thinks like the body, that part travels on. The part that just...exists, that's not tied to a physical aspect of being, that moves on too. So a ghost— that's a third part of the soul, maybe, a purpose or a feeling, a reason for staying. A spirit. And a spirit exists for its purpose," he went on, unable to stop once he'd started, "but what if the purpose is bad, and you draw its notice? Why is it forbidden to call on spirits?"

"Is it forbidden? By whom?"

But Simon was still talking himself in circles. "Most people don't get the chance. And what does calling mean? Is it just divination? Say they've dropped in—could you have a chat? What do you ask then? Do you say hullo? Truth is," he said, bundling his arms against his chest, "there's too many things to say, and it's too big to begin."

"Oh, I see," I said. "You're scared of talking to ghosts because you're scared of talking to everyone."

The corners of his eyes crinkled. "You could put it that way."

"Then I'm sorry, old boy, but you simply won't make it on the spiritualist circuit. Do you suppose any of those frauds are actually magicians? Tap once for yes and twice for no." I knocked on his shoulder. "Forbidden or not, what if I were there to help you? We could hold our own séance next time we're at Uncle Vee's. And we'll take notes, so Muv will have to approve."

"So good to see you!" he said to an imaginary ghost. "And how's the weather in the world to come?"

"That's the spirit," I replied.

His laughter, when it finally came, warmed my cold little heart.

FIVE

AGIC DIDN'T interest me, but Simon did. I marked his progress throughout the beginning weeks of December.

First Muv had him write down every instance of magic he remembered performing, anything that had happened to him or that he felt he'd made happen. She then challenged him to sort these instances into categories of his own devising. For instance, what did he think constituted small magic? Large magic? Was his pulling ace of hearts after ace of hearts from my deck of cards significant, or was it incidental? When he turned every object in our house a slight, beguiling mauve, was it a piece of large magic because it affected a wide area, or small magic because it lasted only five minutes? (Five delightful minutes, in my opinion, which I gave even though no one deigned to ask it.) Was time a pertinent metric? Was space? If they weren't, what were? What qualities, if any, made Simon's magic truly his?

When he answered her with metaphors and poetry,
how the word *amulet* tasted like sunrise, that sort of thing,
I knew he'd started playing her game.

After a week or two of thought experiments, Muv asked
him about enacting magic on purpose.

It was during Simon's subsequent, searching pause that
I wandered into the drawing room and perched on the
arm of an old wing-back chair. I had finished the day's
fencing drills, and my freedom would be all the more
enjoyable for watching someone else squeeze his tender
brain through the wringer.

Go on, I prompted Simon, gesturing. He raised a finger
to his lips, but Muv paid me no mind. It was another
of her difficult days; though she acted more or less like
herself, she hadn't troubled to don more than a loose tea
gown and robe.

"Let me put it another way," she said, tapping her
pen on her journal. "Would acknowledging yourself as
a magician make you feel obligated to put magic to use?
Furthermore: what does *use* mean to you? Is it bettering
yourself? Bettering the world?"

"I first have to ask myself if I *can* use it." When Simon
caught himself fidgeting with a stray thread on the cuff
of his shirt, he folded his hands. "Do I make magic
happen or does it happen to me? If I cause it, then I want
it to have purpose. If I'm witness to it, then it deserves
response."

She fixed him with her butterfly-pinningest gaze.
"Consider what draws magic to you, then. Action,
inaction. Repetitive thoughts, self-scrutiny."

"Things happen if I'm well-behaved or not, I've figured
out that much."

"I shouldn't think you would behave poorly." Flexing
her hands, Muv closed her eyes. Cold, damp weather
never helped the ache.

Mostly to amuse Simon with my benevolence, see, I

could play the good child, I fetched her a hot water bottle.
She swaddled it in a shawl and folded her bare fingers
across it, like a priestess with her esoteric symbol.

"One cannot control magic," she was saying, a
continuation of her lecture from Simon's first day. "Though
the very notion is a lie, we magicians must constantly
persuade ourselves that it is true. We create charms for
ourselves through which we may converse with infinity."
She shrugged. "That is my understanding. It may not be
yours. Given that magic resists any cohesive paradigm, I
must rely upon an example—my own—in order to explain
further. As Julia mentioned to you, I am not well."

Simon and I exchanged sheepish glances.

"I have never been well," Muv coolly went on. "Even
as a child, I was not what one would call *of sound mind*.
When I was about twelve, my father sent me to hospital
for a year, after which I relied on a personal attendant.
I was desperately unhappy. My Koldunov cousins,
meanwhile, were inculcated with an unshakeable belief
that they were special—that their beauty and bloodline
granted them the world. They were magicians. I wanted
a share of the power that came so easily to them." She
inclined her head with wry deference to the facts, as if
to say: I have it now, look where it got me. "I created
rituals for myself, most of them unpleasant, but they
felt meaningful at the time. My methods have since
evolved. Yours will, too. There are as many ways of
relating to magic as there are to a lover, or a parent, or a
meddlesome neighbour."

At least Simon seemed to enjoy these conversations. I
mussed his curls as I passed him, winning a small, weary
sigh, and went to look out the window.

"How do you see magic now?" I heard him ask.

"I am respectful, generally, if respect includes petty
quarrels and deliberate provocation. A time-honoured
tradition." Was that a smile in Muv's voice? I glanced

over my shoulder, but I'd missed it. "I don't think of magic as having emotions, or goals, or interests, certainly not as regards individual beings. I find insignificance reassuring; my actions don't and *cannot* matter to a force beyond human comprehension. And yet—it is for humans I am obligated to act. What I do matters to people, very much. The power is in the contradiction."

"That makes sense," Simon said. And it did, a little, for her. Muv couldn't admit to a paradox and leave it at that, no, she had to palpate the guts of the thing, sound out the viscera, and then encourage you to do the same. Like she did with Simon, whose breath became a touch thick as he admitted, "I'm scared. I get sick to think I'll hurt someone. Not through magic, just that I'll do the wrong thing, somehow, and because I've done it, then my family will suffer the consequences, or my friends. You, or Julia."

I put a hand to my heart. "How kind of you to worry for me!"

"I hope I'm kind," he agreed, more seriously, "but I'm no judge. I don't make the order of the world. Is it silly to think my decisions matter?"

"Do they matter? Such considerations are part of being a magician," Muv said. "You must discover for yourself what manner of practice feels most important to you. Not what you think ought to be important, Simon—what genuinely strikes a chord. For instance: when magic calls upon you, must you respond?"

"I'm not obligated, but I can't ignore it."

I kept my eyes firmly on the car rolling down our street, its shine and its sleek turn. There was no snow yet.

Simon always acted as though Muv's lectures were wisdom handed down from on high. They weren't, but I didn't want to spoil his fun.

Since I was no longer at Marable, Muv could afford a private fencing tutor. Miss Talbot said she might teach me épée and sabre too, for the fun of it, as both school and the women's competitions only offered foil. So much for my stint in Purgatory. Muv must have been tired of having me underfoot while she was trying to study with Simon, but fencing lessons at Miss Talbot's studio for two hours thrice weekly still left me ample time to bother him.

During Hanukkah he went home every night to light candles with his grandparents, and the next day he'd come back with chocolate coins for me, among other gifts. One bright morning, his mother Ruta accompanied him. Muv was at one of her Government meetings when I heard their voices at the front door, Simon's own dulcet tones and a voluble, rather hoarse antiphony. Curious, of course, I made my way to the first floor landing as Simon was insisting his mother didn't have to come inside.

"Who else is going to track mud on their floors? Don't tell me you think I need a calling card, I raised you better'n that." She laughed and let her gaze roam about the front hall. "This is where you're staying, is it? Seen the outside a time or two, never in here. I hope she's treating you as well as you deserve."

"Lady Aloysia is nice," said Simon.

"None of these people are nice. I want to talk to her, where is she?"

"Out, sorry," I said, taking the stairs two at a time on my way down and landing beside Simon with a hop. "Hullo, there."

He took after his mother, clearly. Ruta Wolf was short, lean, and tanned, with familiar velvet dark eyes and dark brown hair, though hers was peppered with grey and cut in a messy shingle. Everything she wore was too big for her, from her round, wire-frame spectacles to her huge overcoat, from her baggy shirt to the men's trousers— were those Simon's?—she'd rolled above her ankles. She had a lit cigarette in one hand and three books under her arm, the complement to Simon's much larger stack.

He'd brought some of his texts from home.

"What's this vile young creature? Here, you'll do. For your mum." With a broad wink she dug into her coat pocket and passed me a fold of paper. "Glad to see my boy's making friends with the wrong people, which reminds me, the Kolskis' youngest asked after you, the one from your boxing club. Hadn't a clue what to say, you'd gone off to live in your ivory tower, abandoning us all—"

"Max spoke to you? About me?" Something in Simon's tone made me think of Charlotte Henley, that mingled resentment and hope, but he wouldn't let us believe he cared too much. "Whatever you said to him was all right, I hope. And you're one to talk! Gran wondered where you were the other night."

"I saw that relic just lately, when you were having your little magic problem."

"Months ago, Ma."

"So I should light some candles with her and Tatty, what more do they want? I won't wear a skirt."

"Gran wonders, is all. She says you don't respect your mother!" said Simon.

"And you respect *your* old Ma, do you?" Ruta countered.

I hated to interrupt an argument they so obviously enjoyed performing for each other, not least because Simon's arguing about anything was a rare spectacle, but I had to ask: "You're exchanging letters with Muv?"

"Her highness remembered me, wasn't I surprised! Not much worth remembering about Vee's parties even if you could, wouldn't blame her if she hadn't. Got the first royal missive when she heard about Si. She's still putting up with Vee?" Ruta snorted. "Can't imagine she'd ever forgive him, but I'm not fool enough to barge into her schemes, except when it comes to Simon. *That* man was a mistake," she said, pinching Simon's ear, "but my baby boy's the best thing I ever did, except the time I landed a rock at Downing Street—and for a demonstration only, they put me in jail! Wasn't the last time, I can tell you, but why the long face, Si? I tease, I tease."

"Forgive him for what?" I asked.

Ruta eyed me as she took a drag from her cigarette. "Sorry, love. That's another one for your mum."

The provoking person's favourite excuse: shouldn't have mentioned it, so sorry, my mistake. A mistake it could have been, but I'd pulled that trick too often to trust anyone else. It was all about the reaction you'd get, and mine hadn't displeased Ruta.

"Tell her I dropped by," she said, adding her three books to Simon's stack. "And don't you work too hard, I don't care what she pays you."

"To make up for me not working at the fish shop," he muttered at my curious look. "I'll see you next week, then, give Millie my love. Ma's friend, Jules, we live with— oof—" Before he could finish, Ruta's hug crushed the breath out of him.

"And why does he want his dear mother to leave? I love you, my boychik." She slapped Simon's back as she withdrew, and then, noticing the cigarette ash on the rug, cheerfully ground it beneath her heel. "Ta ta, kids."

"Cheerio!" The door slammed behind her, and I rounded on Simon. "I like her very much, thank you, but why on earth would she resume contact with Uncle Vee? What did you *do*?"

He blinked into an entirely too sunny smile. "I'll tell you after I put away these books, shall I?" He lifted them, demonstrating their weight.

"Go on, then. Muv will be glad you took her seriously."

He was hoping I would forget I'd asked. I wouldn't, but I was trying to be a good friend; I wouldn't press him. Distressing magical incidents were the sort of thing he confided to Muv, not me, which was all very well, only no one was willing to tell me anything about anything these days.

I sat on the bottom stair and examined Ruta's note. It wasn't sealed. A glance over each shoulder confirmed neither Simon nor Beth and Dolly were about.

A., you splendid bitch, the letter read, *we'll have it out over coffee & buns if you can't bring yourself to feast on the bloated corpse of the bourgeoisie. -R.*

I laughed and pushed it beneath Muv's bedroom door.

SIX

THOUGHT about Simon a great deal while Muv and I visited her father up north at Castle Barrowbeck for Christmas. He would be having a better time with his family than we were.

After my errant grandmother died in her Paris flat—surrounded by picture postcards and empty bottles of scent, I imagined, and the roses bestowed upon her by old flames—Grandad had married again. His second wife, Dismal Dorothy, had also failed to give him an heir. Then, instead of a grandson who could continue something of the family line, my father having agreed to add the Stirling to his children's names, there was only a Julia Grace. I could have married whoever was next to inherit the title, but two generations of Stirling men were rotting away in the Somme or Ypres. If the massive dispute couldn't be solved, the next Earl of Barrowbeck would be nobody at all.

Though I dimly recalled a more volatile fuss when my parents divorced, in response to which Grandad disinherited Muv and married his dull railroad heiress, the war had worn down our family into resignation and bleak scorn.

Everything could have been mere bad luck.

I was terribly restless over Christmas. Muv was, too. She spent her time solidifying patterns she'd first created when she was a little girl. It was tap-tap-tap on every doorknob, tap-tap-tap on certain objects and odd mullioned windows. Even I could gather she'd spun a vast web. *Strangling* was the word that came to mind.

After a ghastly dinner, during which Grandad expressed his displeasure with the food, the company, and society in general, even as Dot blinked back tears and Muv silently quit the table, I tried to lighten the mood by telling school stories. When that backfired, and Grandad turned on me, I too fell silent.

The next evening, Muv passed me a note. She'd used the inverted words I'd copied for her to encrypt an old Tennyson poem, I discovered, once I'd spent an hour or two cracking the cipher. When I got past the symbols and found a mere Caesar shift, I felt indulged, a bit babied, but at least the solution came readily. It was something to keep me occupied as I sat with everyone else in the solar, the only warm room in the castle. Dorothy stopped trying to eke pleasant conversation out of Grandad and Muv when I took pity on her, on all of them, really, and explained the puzzle. Muv watched me carefully but said not a word.

On our return the London house, as grim as it had seemed before, appeared unto me as a bright pinnacle of twentieth century civilisation. Even brighter and better: we would be escorting Simon to the Koldunovs' annual New Year's Eve celebration. Uncle Vee always scheduled it for our calendar date—his event simply *must* be the liveliest of many, not some trifling January party for the Orthodox émigrés.

"This is our opportunity," I told Simon, folding my arms on his shoulder as he examined the invitation I'd dropped onto his open book. "Think about it, do."

"A séance? In the middle of a party?"

"On the early side, to be honest, if we time it to the stroke of midnight. But we'll sneak away!"

"People will get ideas," said Simon.

I pushed my thumb into the frown at the corner of his mouth. Smile! "I know, I know, if you're seen to associate with me it will be terribly shaming. A black mark on your reputation. I may be a notorious rake, but I promise your virtue will remain intact."

He swatted me away and sighed, which meant he'd agree eventually. I didn't mean to press him about it. I just gave him excuses to indulge his curiosity.

The Koldunovs' Kensington house was a bower of opulent taste: potted palms, painted floral walls, an excess of stained glass. It even smelled delicious, like cinnamon and whisky, with a hint of dried roses. As we were removing our winter things, Muv kissed her two gloved fingers and pressed them to a swooping, upturned wooden flower on the grand stair's banister. Simon drew a breath.

"What's she done now," I grumbled, deciding to blame her for the static electricity that had set my hair on end, as though it weren't already wispy enough.

Muv lent me her comb. "I was testing something."

As I examined my dress and stockings for any mysterious rips or stains or tucks that might have appeared on the drive over, two familiar voices pelted me.

"Yule!"

"Yog!"

"Yoolia-woo!"

"Chickens!" I threw myself into the outstretched arms of Marie and Adele.

They were only a year apart in age, fourteen and fifteen, with bobbed brown curls and round blue eyes.

Adele was older and sweeter, but Marie was brighter.
They'd inherited their mother's figure, perfectly suited to
the old pigeon-pout bosoms and cinched waists, but these
days they got by on clever tailoring, as did we all. Even
if I had any bust to speak of, my blue chiffon dress would
have hung just the same, slack from shoulder to knee.
Neither the younger Koldunova girls nor I were supposed
to be more than presentable. None of us were *out*.

Marie and Adele swept me into the party proper,
giggling as I exaggerated about my awful Christmas with
the Stirlings. I didn't forget Simon. I wasn't abandoning
him. I'd come back. Muv could escort him, and I hadn't
seen the Koldunovs in a month. I *couldn't* have forgotten
him. The girls' curiosity didn't allow it.

"What is it like, having him live with you?" asked Adele.

"Pretty well like it was with us, I should imagine," said
Marie. "He was so quiet and odd, not at all how I thought
he'd be, nothing like Papa."

"Simon's all right," I said. "You'd be shy, too, if you'd
been tossed to a squabble of nasty swans." When I
pinched Marie's arm, she pinched me back.

"You're friends with him," accused Marie.

"I'm friends with everybody!"

"Oh, Jules," said Adele. "How charitable you are!"

I looked over my shoulder. Muv and Simon had only
just come around the corner; they wouldn't have heard.

There were fewer White Russians in attendance
than Upper Ten Thousand, who thought the ousted
nobility were marvellously exotic and tragic; the former,
meanwhile, enjoyed the chance to indulge in memories
and vodka. Though the Koldunovs had emigrated much
earlier, in Uncle Vee's father's time—when the tsar had
got wind of what dread horrors Uncle Vee's grandfather
perpetrated vis-à-vis magic and certain death rites, not to
mention the gambling, and exiled the lot of them—there
was enough common feeling over which to imbibe.

These parties had been quite another thing when Uncle Vee was young and wild.

Muv was speaking to Simon in a low voice as he nodded and cast nervous glances at the full drawing room. I hoped he would not melt into the floor; he looked dashing in his dinner jacket and tie, a worthy student of my mother. She wore draped devoré velvet, plain black, it seemed, until the delicate floral patterns rippled into view beneath the blaze of the chandeliers.

Though the the gramophone violins merrily warbled, they were drowned out by the perpetual toasts.

Uncle Vee was already intoxicated enough to peck Muv's lips. All I heard was, "My hazel witch, my queen of thorns," before Muv demanded to know what he'd poisoned himself with this time.

"—and Mama won't let us go see where she killed him," Marie was saying, "so next time your mother's on her rounds, ask if she'll let us come with her to the Savoy."

"Madame Fahmy was so beautiful!" Adele sighed.

"And filthy rich with her husband's money. I can't believe she got off, she shot him three times—"

"Oy, Jules!" I turned to find one fire poker leveled not two inches from my nose, and another shoved into my hand. "En garde!"

Arthur's and my mock duel ended with his crying touché and staggering about as though I'd stabbed his heart. Fencing wasn't his sport; he played rugby for Oxford. Nepotism was the only reason he'd been admitted, and the only reason they let him stay. Oh, Arthur. Blond, hearty, brainless Arthur. As I'd earlier explained to Simon, the odds of his dying from reckless stupidity before he inherited were high enough that everyone pretended he was Uncle Vee's child.

Simon had oozed out a groan and asked whether Arthur knew he had a different father.

"Gosh, no," I'd said, "and don't ever tell him. Let

Joseph goad him into a tragic sailing accident as nature intended."

From the floor, Arthur asked, "Is what's-his-nose here?"

"Simon," I corrected.

"I could take him."

I helped to hoist him off of the rug. "You could try."

"See if I don't, kid." He winked and tweaked my ear. "Ain't you cute this evening. We'll get you some champagne, ring in the New Year with a respectable fizz. What timing! There's the old man now."

Uncle Vee was moving towards us, his cane in one hand and two flutes balanced in the other; but he was waylaid by two elderly ladies, whose rings he kissed, and to whom he graciously presented each glass. He could never resist an opportunity to be charming.

"Where's Aunt Dahlia?" I asked Arthur. "I ought to say hullo before I forget, or she'll never forgive me."

"Can't wait to get away, eh? No, no, go on. Think she's in the library with Gee."

Laughing, I let him dip and spin me off in the right direction. Though I was too short to see over most of the adults, I was slim enough to squeeze between them. To their eyes, I was nothing but a flash of ginger-blonde, a breeze of gauze, a wink of gold off of my new hair slide: a child, and therefore invisible.

I found Aunt Dahlia by their big, prewar family portrait, holding a glass of sherry and speaking too loudly. "Do get a moment with Lord Ashley, dear, he's not unattractive—"

"I will, Mama."

"Don't forget Lord Ivor, either—"

"I haven't, Mama."

"There are so few eligible men, Georgie, a girl can't afford to rest on her laurels. Not even you."

Georgia remained sublimely unperturbed. She was exquisite: glacial blue eyes, long black hair pinned at the nape of her long white neck, silver dress slim about her hips.

Seeing her beneath a portrait of her young father was
all the more uncanny, as though the artist had painted
her into life. Did she know she was magic? Did she bathe
in bull's blood or burn peacock feathers on a golden
altar, or was it unconscious? Perhaps it was a vanity so
strong, reinforced by everything anyone ever said to her,
it coloured reality. Looking at Gee almost hurt, yet I
couldn't stop.

"Jules, sweetheart, come here!" Aunt Dahlia beckoned
me into one of her comfortable hugs before adding, "I've
a present for you. Christmas, you know, from Vee and me,
and the children. I'll fetch it, shall I?—and you stay there,
have a chat with Georgie." Off she fluttered, unaware of
what panic she'd called forth in my giddy heart, but I did
love presents.

"Hullo, Gee." I gave her a winning smile.

"Darling." Pale and smelling of jasmine, she embraced
me. "Expelled, were you?"

"You know me! No wall is high enough to hold our
Jules." I curtseyed. "Ever the prankstress, ever the
troublemaker, entirely at your service."

She smiled. "What a funny girl you are."

Before I had to conjure up a response, I was saved by
the gold-wrapped parcel Aunt Dahlia presented to me.
Within was a bracelet, a dainty geometry of yellow topaz
and real diamonds. Naturally, I gasped. "This is too
much, this is too, too much. No one's given me jewels of
my own, not even Muv, only pearls. Oh, thank you!" Aunt
Dahlia fastened it around my wrist as I beamed.

"There! I doubt Aloysia will approve of your wearing it,
but even she can make an exception for tonight."

After I thanked her yet again, at once delighted and
ready to die beneath the moon that was Georgia's cool,
benevolent smile, I felt it was high time I found my way
back to Simon. A funny girl, was I? I had to leave before
the *little* got wedged in.

I passed a group of middle-aged Russian men tossing back shots of vodka with a couple of overwhelmed peers' sons, who received many sturdy claps on the back; I snared a glass of champagne from my old pal Tom the driver, drafted into wait service for the evening, who sighed and shook his head but did not stop me; and I flashed my wrist at Muv, who released a deep breath. For this party she'd got her own diamonds from the bank, and there they glittered on her pale, freckled sternum.

She was talking with several men I recognised, barely, as ministers and diplomats for whom she'd enacted magic during the war. Rumour had it she'd been an interrogator, an intelligence operative, a negotiations expert—or a very clever charlatan who'd blackmailed her way into a Government salary, but no one here believed she was a fraud. They'd witnessed firsthand what she could do, these fellows, though I suspected much of it hadn't been to their liking. If they thought she followed directives without an agenda of her own, they didn't know the Lady Aloysia. Such great heroes they were, statesmen shouldering their medals, yet all of them were diminished by the small, solitary woman at their side.

I quickly changed directions, thank you. I had no desire to be introduced.

Simon stood in a corner, pretending to examine a bookshelf as he struggled for conversation with my least favourite Koldunov sibling, including Lizzie. Joseph might have lacked the preternatural sparkle of his father and eldest sister, but he was very much in their mould. You could believe he and Simon were half-brothers if you already knew. Perhaps that was why Jos had made his way over, either to investigate the new blood, see how it held up, or to show off what he thought were his superior looks.

Simon seemed unaware there was a competition.

"Having fun, Julia?" Simon said, but I heard: Julia, thank goodness. I'm drowning, Julia, I'm floundering without a lifeboat. I will perish in icy waters, Julia. Save me, Jules.

I tossed my head. "A queen must attend to her court."

"I see you're in top form tonight," said Jos.

"As though you're one to judge," I shot back. "My form, or any girl's."

"I think you have the girls pretty well covered."

"Darling Jos," I replied, "no one is spared from my discerning eye."

"Of course it landed on Gee again, but that's to be expected. You're a free woman now." Jos loftily pushed up his spectacles. "I heard you and Char Henley had a tiff. She's going with Siddy Callahan-Waite."

"Splendid," I said, "unless you had a claim on him?"

"With those ears of his? I would sooner die."

Our homosexual proclivities were one thing Jos and I had in common, at any rate, though he knew I wasn't necessarily opposed to boys. No matter whether Jos confused Simon or scandalised him, the intention was the same: to make him feel how thoroughly he did not belong. He was silent, yes, and wary, but Jos had missed the mark. Given his blush when Ruta mentioned his friend Max, I suspected Simon had more of a stake in this conversation than he'd let on.

I took his arm. "Has Jos been heckling you, too?"

"We were talking about school," said Jos. "A subject on which you cannot possibly have anything to add."

"Oh, of course—there is no *true* school but Eton."

"How old are you, again?" Simon asked. When Jos answered that he was seventeen, Simon raised his eyebrows and sipped his wine. I did so enjoy when Jos got the set-downs he deserved.

"Done any magic tricks recently?" Jos didn't even try to suppress the twitch of his upper lip. "Though I suppose Lady A whipped you into shape."

"I thought you were above magic," I said.

"Doesn't mean I can't ask Mr. Wolf how he's been getting on. I heard when he was here last, he couldn't do anything out of the common way. *So* disappointing for everybody, I'm sure."

"Jealous, are you? He's done loads of magic with us," I said, and Simon returned my smile.

As if summoned by this talk of magic, Uncle Vee joined our circle. With his silver cuff links, his tails and tie, his black silk lapels as smooth as his hair, he was everything dapper and distinguished, a vision of heartbreaking grace. He swept us a bow. Jos affected boredom, Simon stopped himself from hunching his shoulders, and I greeted Uncle Vee with a chipper, "I already told Aunt Dahlia, but thank you for the present!"

"Let's have a look, then," said Uncle Vee, and I presented my arm with a flourish, not expecting that he'd gently take my hand. "Ah, yes. There's nothing like a bracelet to set off a slender wrist, is there?" He dropped a kiss on my knuckles and let go.

"Muv wasn't best pleased with your giving it to me." I followed Simon's gaze to where she stood, the magician among her ministers, and remembered what he'd said about the world dancing along her lines.

She looked Simon in the eye, tilted her head and, with a single, sharp tug of her glove, turned her back.

Uncle Vee didn't notice. "I expect she's of the opinion you're not old enough, but never mind that, Georgie had jewels at your age. Are *you* pleased?"

"It's very beautiful. Isn't it, Simon? Jos?"

"You may as well be our sister," said Jos. "You're obnoxious enough."

His *our* did not include Simon, who exhaled heavily through his nose. I felt very awkward and warm all of a sudden, as though Simon disapproved of me, but that couldn't be right. I hadn't done anything. Uncle Vee believed his attention was an indulgence, a precious treat.

In the moment, it always was.

After another long sip of wine, Simon spoke. "Sir. We were just talking about the progress I've made with Lady Aloysia."

"Were you, then?" Uncle Vee glanced from one lovely son to the other. Jos smirked, certain he'd somehow triumphed when his father fondly clapped his shoulder and said to Simon, "Do let's hear."

I'd stepped half apart from them already when Marie and Adele whisked me away for a round of Murderer's Hole (wherein we decided who at the party would commit murder, why, how they'd accomplish the deed, and whether or not they'd be clever enough to get away with it). I would thank Simon later for whatever he thought he'd done, though I did recognise how difficult it was for him to face Uncle Vee. Brave Si! I resolved to blame neither him nor Muv for sullying a perfectly usual exchange. If Uncle Vee was overbearing and ridiculous, the two of them were paranoid.

Thirty minutes before midnight, Simon found the girls and me leaning over the grand stair's glossy banister, olives in our hands and mischief in our hearts. Before he could refuse, I popped an olive into Simon's palm.

"You aim for the adults' drinks," I said, and demonstrated.

The olive bounced to the floor, where it was crushed beneath mean old Grand Duke Mikhail Mikhailovich's foot. Marie, Adele, and I chorused our dismay. Then we turned to Simon.

"Have any of you ever succeeded?" he asked, sceptical.

"Once," said Marie, and Adele added, "That was how the game started. Papa was so impressed he joined the fun. Where is he, I wonder—do you suppose he'll see?"

"Are you going to disappoint us, Simon?" I asked.

Of course he could not withstand three expectant stares. Sighing, he pitched his olive towards the upheld

glass of a balding, bearded gentleman. It struck the
man's head with an almost audible *twock!*—and when he
looked around, the girls and I, giggling, ducked behind
the banister. Simon was left to gaze at the ceiling. What,
who, me? He carried it off well, he and his fawn's eyes, his
worried brow: a regular ingénue.

As we unfolded ourselves from our crouch, Simon said,
"You still on, Jules?"

"Oh *my*," said Marie. Adele continued giggling.

"Hush," I scoffed, "it's nothing like that. We're going to
hold a séance, pester some of the family ghosts."

"Do be careful, Jules, you'd be too, too nice a corpse,"
said Adele, readying another olive.

Marie ate one of hers. "Tell us any good stories."

On our way up the stairs, I was pleased to inform
Simon he'd made a favourable impression on Marie and
Adele. See! The girls could be won over. They were his
sisters, and they were my friends. It was only right these
three should like each other as much as I liked them, but
never mind me, what did Simon think of the Koldunov
siblings now?

"I don't know," he said. "Flock to their father, don't
they?"

"If you'd grown up with him, you would too." Heavy
warmth swept from my chest to my cheeks.

Simon had to have seen my discomfort, but with no
more acknowledgement than a slight cock of his head, he
changed the subject—"Well, where are we headed?"—
and I let myself perk right up.

I had been pondering the best place from which to
summon spirits. Anywhere in the Koldunov house would
net us someone, I was sure, but you never knew whether
ambiance might contribute to the magic. Since Simon
liked books, I decided to bring him to a library study, the
one where Uncle Vee and Aunt Dahlia kept their racy
literature too blatantly hidden. The party noise faded.

The creaks began. Except for lily-belled sconces at long intervals, the lights were off.

Lizzie ought to have given us a fright, as ghostly as she looked in her nightdress, but we did see her from all the way down the hall.

"You're supposed to be asleep," I said, stopping where she stood.

"I am *not*."

"Hullo, Lizzie." Simon wasn't good with children but desperately thought he should be. He knelt on one leg and slung his arm over the other. "Remember me?"

"Yes." Plump, sullen Lizzie was a long way yet from her siblings' swanhood. Her glare was fierce beneath brows too heavy for her babyish face. She kept mouthing pieces of her tangled black hair as her nose dribbled; the slime and saliva had coalesced into a wet sheen on her upper lip.

Simon glanced up at me. "Doesn't she have, er, a nanny?"

"Sometimes, but the last one was sacked for teaching Marie and Adele how to shoplift." I shrugged. "You can take care of yourself, can't you, Lizard mine?"

"It's misses and misters," she said around her hair.

"What's that?" Simon leaned in.

"I'm going to *see* my misses and *misters*."

I made a face. "We don't know what that means."

Simon stood and said, "Let's get you back to your room, eh?" Looking at me: "We can't take her with us."

Lizzie, closing her damp hand around his wrist, begged to disagree.

I imagined what would happen if Simon and I made ourselves responsible for putting Lizzie to bed. She'd raise a fuss, we'd grow impatient and get Aunt Dahlia, who would scold Simon or worse, and Simon would feel terrible, and I would feel terrible for him, and then Lizzie would sense how terrible everybody felt and start to cry.

"Perhaps," I said slowly, "perhaps her presence will help. She's named for one of the ghosts, after all. There could be magic in that." I was hoping Lizaveta the First would be the one to grant Simon an audience, though I'd also settle for Muv's blonde ghost.

Less for Lizzie's welfare than for the sake of his own anxiety, not wanting to break a rule or anger the family, Simon protested, "It's late."

"It's New Year's! Everybody will be too knackered tomorrow to notice her."

Simon grimaced but followed me towards the library study. Lizzie clung to him and chewed her hair with a determination that transcended intent.

As the first one inside the study, I turned on the stained glass desk lamp. It cast a rosy glow onto the walls, a hypnotic shimmer; one of Aunt Dahlia's and Uncle Vee's artist friends had painted a mural of golden flowers. Gilt-framed, photographic portraits of Uncle Vee's erstwhile paramours cluttered the desk. Among the men and women I couldn't name, I found a pretty, luxuriant Aunt Dahlia and a nearly-unrecognisable Ruta Wolf, her hair piled up like a mushroom cap. And, yes—there were several pictures of my young mother. Her tidy little face was much like mine, though her brows were stronger, her mouth harder, her eyes colder, as if she scorned the viewer for looking back at her across all those years. She hadn't thought it would be me.

Lizzie crawled onto an armchair and rubbed her hands across the velvet. Freed of his dribbly shackle, Simon stood with his arms folded. The shadows cut his cheekbones quite, quite marvellously.

I said so, and then laughed at his flustered, "Shut up, Jules."

"I shall be your secretary," I continued, sitting behind the desk and opening what few drawers were unlocked.

A pen was easy to find; paper, less so. Could I write in
the margins of very bad pornography? Desecrate a lewd
poem? But at last I was able to dig out some of Uncle Vee's
monogrammed stationery. My preparations complete, I
tipped my chin at Simon and blinked prettily. "Well?"

He pointed at a clock. "If we're trying for the stroke
of midnight, I've got ten minutes to come up with
something."

"You've had days and days! Remember what Muv said,
about magic being what feels meaningful to you. Are
there any Jewish New Year's traditions?"

"I shouldn't like them for this. And ours was in
September."

"Drat." I tapped the pen on the table. "You've nothing
at all? No ideas?"

Lizzie was kicking her heels on the armchair, watching us.

"How would you summon a ghost, Jules?"

"Same as I'd summon anybody else. Introduce myself,
ask nicely for the pleasure of their company, or bribe them
with a favour. What would a ghost want?"

"That we could give?" Simon turned his palms
upward, at a loss. "Conversation?"

"A listening ear!" I took note of our deliberations.
"Very good. Try that. Do we have any herbs we can
burn? I ate my olives."

"There are no candles," said Simon, exasperated, and
then—I could see it, the very moment he resolved to take
this seriously. To find out what happened when he acted
first, instead of waiting until magic inevitably called upon
him. "If we had salt, we could sprinkle it in a circle. Think
a circle of books would do?"

I doubted the quality of ghost he'd get, given the
literature in question, but we laid out a good twenty books
on the floor in a vaguely circular shape. I returned to the
desk, and Simon remained standing. All the while Lizzie
had been talking to herself in the way children would do,

breathy whistles and clucks.

"Excellent sound work, keep it up," I said, in response to which she bit her finger and frowned.

"One minute to midnight." Simon cleared his throat. "Any ghosts who are listening, er, we're here. Hullo?" When I raised my eyebrows at him, he gave a little laugh and composed himself. He breathed. This time his voice was smoother, his shoulders straight. "Spirits of this family and this house," he began, "I, Simon Wolf, apprentice magician, son of Ruta Wolf—here with my companions, Miss Julia Selwyn-Stirling and Miss Lizaveta Vladimirovna Koldunova—request your presence at the turning of this year."

As the clock struck midnight, he bowed.

"Impressive," I said, and it was; the hair on my arms stood on end. "See anything?"

He shook his head at me. The clock continued to chime.

Lizzie stopped prodding the upholstery. "Oh," she said, and as neutral and arch as a six-year-old could possibly be, added: "I don't care for that man."

"Who—Simon?"

"I think she means the ghost," he said. The nerves had caught him up.

I peered at Lizzie, who remained unconcerned. "There's another magician in the family, then. Naughty Liz, you've been holding out on us! But that does explain her misses and misters. Who's this one?"

The clock continued to chime.

"Nikolai, did you say his name was? The man with the exploded face and chest," Simon clarified. "Lizzie, you should cover your eyes."

She did, but when Simon turned around again, she peeked through her fingers.

"Prince Nikolai Nikolaevich," he went on. "Sir. I ask a sign that you understand and acknowledge your—your nephew."

Simon seeming to talk to thin air would have been laughable, and a bit pathetic, if it weren't entirely eerie. Pen at the ready, I asked, "What's he doing?"

"He's mouthing a word, I think. I'm not sure which. One syllable." Simon frowned. "And for your notes— he's got jerky movements, and he repeats them like he's performing a routine. Like a cuckoo clock that's stuck. He puts a hand to his head, glances at the blood on his fingers, hand to the heart. He turns his head to you, and then turns his head to Lizzie. He only looked at me when I asked him for a sign."

"What a snob. Ask him why he killed Lizaveta Nikolaevna." I paused. "Sorry, Lizzie. I probably wasn't supposed to say that."

"I don't know what anybody's talking about," she grumbled. "I don't like it."

"I can't just *ask* him why he killed his sister," said Simon. "Did he? Never mind. No. All right." He breathed. "Prince Nikolai Nikolaevich, how did you die?"

"It's obvious, isn't it?" I mimed a blast at my face and chest.

"Julia! That's not what I meant."

"So ask him what you do mean," I retorted.

And the clock continued to chime. Long past twelve, it rang on, rang on and on. Static electricity raced through my hair. I could hardly pat it down as I wrote.

Our Simon puts on a grand show when he tries, I scribbled, suspecting he was almost enjoying this. The more complicated emotions would arise later.

"Prince Nikolai Nikolaevich, you will hear your brother's son." His gesture had something of Uncle Vee's grace. "Who caused your death?"

"Why did you put it like that?" I asked.

Simon shrugged.

Lizzie, who soaked up all of Marie's and Adele's murder stories and was used to this sort of talk, poor child, watched with growing impatience. She didn't like this one; we ought to have summoned another ghost more pleasing to her fancy. I wondered, suddenly, whether she'd foreseen our purpose when she went wandering.

The clock chimed.

Simon paused, waited. Then he said, "Near as I can tell, he's saying *her*. And *him*. There's a lot of mess. Lizzie, stop looking."

I did not want to feel what I was feeling. I did not want to suspect what I suspected. I did not want to know what I had always known.

"His arm's caught, like it's on a pulley. I think he's trying to point. Could you turn around some of those photographs, Jules?"

One by one, I faced the frames outward. Though I debated whether to save the culprits for last, the dramatic reveal, the postponement of whatever emotion I was determined not to experience, I supposed Simon, too, had worked out whom they'd be.

The picture was of them on a velvet couch, my mother and Uncle Vee. He was beautiful and languid; Muv was not. How strange it was, seeing her with dishevelled curls and lace skirts, more doll than girl. Her hand was caught in Uncle Vee's, her neck stiff beneath his fingers' slim curve. They must have sat for an ambitious photographer friend, as there was an attempt to be artistic about the shadows and light. When I moved my wrist, my bracelet flashed at me. I covered it so tightly the jewels dug into my palm.

"Horrid clock," I said as it chimed into the silence.

I wanted to shove aside Simon's face for how sympathetically he was looking at me. He was too nice to ask whether I'd got what I wanted. Instead he said, "They'll have had a reason."

"Obviously."

Further communication would wait. Confronted with a bloody ghost, a yawning Lizzie with her hands over her ears, and a suddenly lackluster me, Simon picked up a book and opened it to a random page. "Prince Nikolai Nikolaevich." In a firm, clear voice he recited a few lines of what I presumed was Hebrew, entirely from memory, and finished with, "Your business is concluded. I bid you goodnight." He clapped shut the book.

The clock stopped.

The door opened. Muv was alone. She stood as straight and slim as a needle, a woman sharp enough to pierce your eye. I noticed the few strands of white in her red hair, the fine lines amidst her freckles. How many threads had she been tracking this evening? How many strings had she pulled? How many people had unwittingly walked into her web?

She expressed nothing of whatever she felt, nothing but a sigh at small Lizzie awake so late. And though she knew perfectly well, she asked: "What are you doing?"

SEVEN

OVER THE next week, Muv avoided answering
our real question by plying Simon with dozens
of her own. Had the summoning of the ghost
been intentional? Yes? What had intent felt like, in both
a physiological and psychological sense? Was the speech
element for my benefit as an observer? How did an
audience change his practice?

"If you don't know, then say so," Muv would remind
him. "Don't make up an answer because you think there
ought to be one."

What had he said to the ghost? The Hebrew phrases, I
learned, were part of Psalm 91. Neither Muv nor I could
immediately place it. She'd spent too many years resenting
Grandad and her Anglo-Catholic upbringing; as for me,
to say I'd paid scant attention in my religion courses was
a vast understatement. I had to dig out a great-aunt's old
Bible so Muv could look up the translation.

"*Thou shalt not be afraid for the terror by night; nor for the
arrow that flieth by day*," she quoted. "Will explaining the

significance clarify why you were drawn to it?"

"It's said at burials and other times. Morning prayers. On certain days."

"Have you consulted a rabbi about your magic?"

"A few," Simon said. "Their opinions differed."

"Understandable. You might experiment further with magic and performance."

At dinner several days later, she asked Simon what he thought about having stopped all of the clocks in the Koldunov house. Their housekeeper had consulted three craftsmen on the matter, and each time had received the same reply: though every clock ought to be in working order, not one of them could be made to budge from precisely 12 o'clock. Aunt Dahlia was terribly put out.

"I am not scolding you," Muv added. "I am curious."

I tented my fingers and batted my eyelashes at him.

He ate a piece of cherry tart at me, and when I replied with a discreet tap of my upper lip, he licked off the smear of cream there before saying, "I'm not sure. I tried to cause something to happen, to make a ghost manifest, and it did. I can take credit, I suppose, but all this time things have happened to me without my doing the work."

Muv smiled as she watched Simon swirl sherry around his glass.

"I experience magic without deliberately causing magic," he said. "But I also pray without expectation that the prayer gets answered. It's all without a point, but it's never pointless. It's like Job, right—I don't decide what happens to me. The kind suffer, the wicked thrive, and God doesn't dispense justice. But you do good because you have the freedom not to. You do it because you can't expect reward. So I shouldn't ask *why does this happen?*— the question is *what do I do?*"

They were getting to me, these dreadful magicians; I actually understood what Simon meant. Still, I wondered, "How do the ghosts fit in?"

He hummed. "If I try to explain their presence—you know, if I've got some sixth sense or I can see ley lines or magnetisms—it makes them less real. I can't remember when I started to see. I believed they existed, so they did. The act of believing in ghosts is the same thing as the result of seeing ghosts, and vice versa. It's like a deed is the result of the deed's result. Magic says things about reality I can hardly explain, but then where can wisdom be found?"

With the soaring chime of metal on porcelain, Muv laid her knife across her empty plate. "Would you say your faith is inseparable from your magic?"

This time without pause, he replied, "Yes."

And then both of them looked so pleased over what to me seemed obvious from the very first. But nobody had said it, had they? Their satisfaction was less about the answer, and more about Simon's confidence. For him, to study Judaism was to be a magician; he'd decided it was true, so truth it was.

I'd never have managed an interest if I'd still been at school. I'd have been occupied with my own problems. Charlotte's doings were of less than no concern to me now, not even her inevitable falling-out with Sid. No matter where I was, my active mind was a curse. I could not leave well enough alone.

During our respective boxing and fencing drills— which Miss Talbot insisted I do every day, even at home, and which were far more fun with Simon around—I was either distracted or too intense. I'd achieve that perfect balance within myself, my foil a true extension of my arm, my body a thing of deadly grace, and I'd ruin it all by lashing out at an innocent chair.

"Maybe you should talk to her," Simon said when I threw my foil to the floor yet again.

"I'd rather fall on my own sword," I brightly replied. "I've a better idea."

He listened to it, sighed heavily, and against his better judgment decided to indulge me. She was my mother, not his; even if I was wrong, which I wasn't, I had the right to lead. After we had a quick wash and changed back into our nice knitted things, we went downstairs.

The ballroom's tall hardwood doors were locked, of course. Muv was out for the day, frightening her ministers and freshening her city wards. We were not to expect her until after dinner. As a token of her esteem, Muv had bestowed Simon with a key. He'd also learned a complicated series of knocks and taps, a ritual of Muv's he performed as a polite acknowledgement of her space. If it had felt like anything, he said, it would've been like pulling a hole in his jumper without unravelling any of the yarn, and then crawling through. When he opened the door, I had a sudden urge to peel cobwebs from my skin, a gossamer itch.

The ballroom kept its shining parquet floor, its columns and its chandeliers, enough of its character that I could picture Jane Austen ladies bouncing about between the lengthy tables. The long, low shelves were crowded with books, journals, glass thermometers, compasses and sextants, callipers, measuring instruments of all sorts. Above them Muv had put up maps of cities, countries, seas and stars, the unfathomable connections between them represented by pinned and knotted threads. Though individual spaces were buried beneath a geologic age of clutter, the room as a whole was sparser than a magician's laboratory had any right to be.

Simon was sucked into the orbit of his work. Muv had given him a table to himself, which he'd piled with his books and more papers, and funny diagrams he covered when I tipped my head to see. He smiled his apology and shrugged.

Apropos of privacy, he said, "She'll know we've been in here. I know you know that, I'm only saying it again."

"Then perhaps *she* will start this conversation we're doomed to have."

"If you want my opinion—"

"Always," I promptly said.

"I think she's waiting for you to come to her. She knows what you're thinking, sure, but she refuses to burden you with all this unless you either ask outright or give her a sign. She cares about you, Jules."

I made a noise of disgust. "Our investigating ought to be sign enough."

Simon watched me as I began pulling journals from the shelves.

"She's arranged them by date," I said, paging through a journal that covered only March and April of 1917. Most of her records were from the war. I knelt before the leftmost shelf and found the beginning: one journal each for 1896 through 1899, and one likewise ordinary volume for 1900, the year Nikolai was killed. When I opened it and turned the pages outward to show Simon—"Now help me decipher wee Muv's hieroglyphs"—several photographs and picture postcards slipped to the floor.

"This one," Simon said suddenly, picking up a photograph. "It's the blonde woman. The ghost." From the back he read, "*To My Dear Miss, from Eileen Dempsey, February 1900.*"

When Simon offered me a look, I slotted the other memorabilia between the pages, all in a thick wad, and traded him the journal for the photograph. The woman was blonde, certainly, as blonde as a person could be, that thin, pale hair pulled back from a hawkish nose and hollow cheeks. Both her plain dress and her tanned, freckled skin seemed too small for her bones. I decided I would have liked her.

"Muv mentioned having an attendant when she was young, someone who helped her. That must be Eileen. Why is her ghost hanging about?"

"Maybe she wants to help us," said Simon, too distracted to state more than the obvious. He was at his desk, frowning over the journal. "This part, here—she wrote out one line over and over, for three pages. Not that I can read any of it. In Greek, is it? Or Russian."

"Her penmanship was awful," I agreed.

"Does this look like Cyrillic?" He waved me over. "I'm not sure it's actually in a different language. She might've used an alphabet as code."

I settled my chin on my hands and pointed as he flipped the pages. "These letters are Greek, but you're right—she's done a substitution cipher, except she hasn't matched alpha to the letter A and so on. Otherwise there'd be more epsilons."

"Oh, yes. You know about ciphers." Luckily for him, and smart too, Simon did not go so far as to say *like mother, like daughter*. His thinking it was bad enough.

Instead he proposed magic.

"I could crack it if you gave me an hour," I protested, lest Simon doubt my ability, though he and I both knew if there were any work involved in our investigation, I'd rather he do it. And who was I to stop his exploratory impulses?

After he cleared a space on his table, Simon laid down the journal, closed, with Eileen Dempsey's portrait tucked beneath the cover. Next he brought out his own deck of cards, shuffled them, and tucked them one by one between each page: the king of clubs, the queen of spades, the ace of hearts, and so on.

He pushed up his sleeves and poised his hands over the journal. He was the grand magician, the courtly gentleman who pulled roses from his extra-dimensional sleeves, who kissed the hand of fate and swept a bow to the ineffable mysteries of the beyond. Slowly, he embraced this version of himself as he spoke.

"I, Simon Wolf, magician and student of the Lady Aloysia Stirling, here with her daughter, the irrepressible

Miss Julia Selwyn-Stirling, in the name of justice, wisdom, and love, do hereby ask you to do with us what you will."

I watched the journal so intently, half expecting it to bloom into lilies or break into spiders, I missed the actual change until I heard Simon laugh. I looked up.

The ballroom went on forever. Truly forever, as far as I could tell, the sort of enormity in which time and space gave up and became the same thing. The door was lost beyond the horizon's subtle curve; the walls and fireplaces, the big window and the shelves, repeated into infinity. Even the work tables had multiplied, each of them in a different configuration: a maze.

I turned to Simon. "Job, was it? If this is God testing you, I can't imagine how you're meant to pass."

"That's not the point, and you know it." He laughed again, more nervous than his words suggested. "I can't think your mother will be too pleased."

"She's the one who gave you the key." When I started walking towards where the door had been, Simon hurriedly grabbed the journal and followed. "It's Bluebeard all over again; she'll have expected something like this. Perhaps it's a lesson! You must remember to tell her everything you observe."

Simon considered this.

"See?" I said. "You wouldn't put it past her."

"I'd rather not lose her trust." He squeezed through a pair of work tables pushed too close together. "You'll roll your eyes at me, but I admire Lady Aloysia."

Instead of giving him the opinion he'd already divined, I climbed onto another table and stood. The repeating chandeliers dwindled to pinpoint stars; the tables at the end of my sight shrank to insects' furniture. I lost count of the fireplaces, of the heavy red curtains and the light that leaked from behind them. There was a thought.

"Let's pull open every curtain we pass," I said, hopping down. "That may give us a better sense of how far we've travelled."

"Or stop us feeling like we're going nowhere."

Unsurprisingly, the garden view also repeated. January was bleak.

After a few curtains, Simon opened his mouth; and though I waited patiently for whatever was going to come out, he rode the pause to its natural end and said nothing. He stared at Muv's journal instead of facing me.

I was ready to sail past him, all's well and good, don't mind me, when he finally managed the fateful words: "About your mother."

I couldn't blame him. It was, I told myself, the very reason we were here.

"The ghost pointed at both of them," he said. "Her and, er, Prince Vladimir."

"Muv knows what people are thinking. She can make them do things."

Simon watched me too soulfully, like he felt he had to act out his sympathy. "So can he, in his way. Why would they cause Nikolai's death? As revenge for his killing Lizaveta? And if he did kill her—not much of an *if*, he probably did it—why? What is it you're looking for here?"

"Eileen must come into it." I pushed past a table.

"But will you be satisfied with solving an old puzzle? I wouldn't be," he said, keeping pace with me. "I think about what Ma's said, what Lady Aloysia deliberately hasn't—the way he acts—"

My cheeks burned. "You don't have to be gentle."

The cobweb itch on my arms came back. The whole, horrible long room was a mausoleum, too quiet. And— unless my eyes deceived me, it was narrower than it had been before. Muv's need to measure things was not without a certain sense. Thank goodness she wasn't here. Either she'd be vexed with what Simon's magic had done to her sanctum or, worse, she'd like it all too well and keep us cataloguing the vagaries of the cosmos until dawn.

She certainly would have agreed with Simon when he said, "Prince Vladimir isn't a good person." Well, no. He wasn't. "Couldn't feel much for him if I tried. Is that selfish? But his whole act must have been pretty irresistible. It's like Lady Aloysia said. He and his brother really, genuinely believed they deserved anything they wanted."

"What does that have to do with Muv?"

"Anything they wanted. Anyone." Simon's eyes held a sad rebuke: Don't make me do this on my own. "That's why she protects you."

"From what? Why?"

"Come on, Jules. She's your mother."

And because she was my mother, I had to be the one to say it.

"All right," I muttered in a horrible, flat, unfamiliar voice, wishing I had my foil. I kicked at a table instead. "Uncle Vee was engaged to her. She was very young, and she was unhappy, and I know he took advantage of her, I *do* listen. He did things he shouldn't have, whether or not she wanted them done. I've seen how he acts. I'm not ignorant. I know. I *know*." I had always known. "He still thinks she belongs to him, and she doesn't. She never did. Just because she was promised to his brother first—" I swallowed. "She was their cousin, their little sister's best friend."

"She wanted to be a magician."

"And Nikolai's ghost kissed her," I whispered.

I didn't know what to do with my hands, which seemed like two hands too many right about then, so I shoved them into my elbows and stood there, scowling, watching Simon want to comfort me. He wouldn't, of course, not until I let him. He was far too kind for the likes of us.

"No one talks about it," I said. "No one talks about *him*."

"No," Simon agreed.

We were in the midst of understanding why not. No one enjoyed feeling this uncomfortable, this heavy, this sad. This was exactly why I hated to think about anything I couldn't make into a joke.

This was what everyone talked around, what no one ever could explain.

The walls, I decided, affording them my haughtiest glare, had almost certainly crept inwards. Or had the furniture proliferated? Perhaps it was both. However it was the forces of the universe had seen fit to inconvenience their supplicants, a fleet of empty tables now crowded before us, so numerous that Simon and I could scarcely wedge ourselves through the spaces between them.

"They were never good people, they couldn't be." Simon's voice was soft. "I think no one's born wicked. But they can grow up thinking the world owes them fealty."

Our footsteps echoed. Though we did our best with the curtains, windows started to appear less and less often. We ducked beneath tables until it became too difficult, and then we scrambled on top of them, or hopped onto one side and swung our legs to the other.

"He told me the magic came from him," Simon said, with an uncharacteristic note of anger. "I hated that, how he wanted me to do something he could claim as *his*, but at least it was an answer. I was coming to terms with it, or—I was trying. And then Lady Aloysia told me there are only questions."

With a heavy sigh, he lowered himself onto a table's edge, holding the journal in his lap. His shoulders sank as he bent his dark, curly head. There was something awfully tender about the way he blinked—a person's eyelashes hadn't ought to be that long. His legs hung over our last glimpse of the floor before the tables shut it out.

It was probably still a floor.

I sat beside him. "Tell me what happened. Why did your mother feel like she had to bring you to Uncle Vee's attention?" And consequently, I thought, to mine and Muv's. Propping my arm on his shoulder, I said, half into my elbow, "Was it so very terrible, what you did?"

"I vanished."

I leaned forward to look up into his face. "You did what?"

Simon drew a deep breath. "My gran's been ill. She and Tatty don't live far, but they don't like to go out. I'd wanted to go for the holidays, only they asked Ma too. I'm very stupid, I said a day wouldn't hurt her, and was it so bad if they make amends?"

I remembered Christmas, Muv's silence at meals with Grandad and Dismal Dot, how I tried so valiantly and in vain to be amusing. "You felt like you had to fix it, but you couldn't."

"It's not been easy for her, getting along. It wasn't just that she wore trousers or cut off her hair." He ventured a glance at me, as though I of all people were one to judge Ruta for going with women. "It's not so awful of me to want her and them both. But I asked, why'd she have to be so—so contrary? She got furious, of course."

With Simon? The darling child, the perfect boy? Though it must have been hard on him, living up to that sort of thing. I wouldn't know, of course, I'd made certain no one thought me a perfect darling, but at school I saw it all the time. Be good, follow the rules, and claim your reward: a life of being good and following rules, as though your virtue could somehow protect you from harm.

"What happened?" I prompted. "What did you do?"

"I don't know. Stalked off, walked away." Another breath steadied him. "I left, I think, to cool my head. But I can't say. I was vanished, gone. Two weeks and four days, before Rosh Hashanah to the middle of Sukkot. I don't remember anything," he added, preempting my inevitable question. "Nothing to remember. Everyone asked, and then they kept asking, of course I was scared and sorry. How could I tell them how I felt? I liked it, not knowing.

Max didn't believe me, and then he thought I'd gone mad. Probably everyone does, but he was so gentle and kind. Why don't I speak with the rabbi, why don't I see a doctor? Everyone was so concerned, there were search parties, and then I came back. Of course there's things I can't say. I could've been or done anything. That time was mine. It was magic." He put his face in his hands. "So all I've done is spite Ma. Well, she'll shrug off what I can't."

I hugged his arm. I'd not be another person who'd ask and ask when he'd already trusted me with his answer.

If it would take the pressure off, ease his discomfort, I'd trust him in return, enough to say, "I wish I could disappear for Stirling family holidays. Grandad doesn't think school is necessary for girls, you know, our sort. It didn't stop him demanding to know why I'd been *sent away*."

"Sounds like an arse."

"He is." My stocking had ripped over the knee; I dragged my nail over the banded threads. "I was such a clever girl, that's what Grandad said. Why did I have failing marks in every single subject? So I told him I was clever enough that I didn't need to prove it to anyone. It sounded bold and all that, but wasn't exactly true. What if I did try, and I wasn't as clever as I thought I was? I didn't mention this to him, but the headmistress would've given me another chance if it weren't for the rest. I was simply *unsuited* to Marable's *particular* academic environment."

"Oh, Jules."

My smile lacked its usual electricity. "This is the first time I've had to explain myself out loud."

The ceiling soared, as lofty as ever; a line of countless chandeliers twinkled both in front of us and behind. There were no more windows, no columns or shelves. No papers, no compasses or sextants. No maps. And the floor over which my restless feet dangled did indeed seem less *there* than I would have hoped.

I bit my lip. "Two weeks, you said?"

"I hope not," Simon replied with a little laugh as he pushed himself upright. He strode across the gap and onto the seamless parquet of tables, a pattern that stretched into space beyond time. I did not particularly want to enter the vaunted planes of abstract mathematics—given my prior encounters with maths, I was doubtful of the welcome I'd receive—but I'd follow our Simon anywhere. I got up.

When he gave Muv's journal a gentle toss, all the playing cards he'd put between the pages spilled out, a constellation of slick rectangles across gleaming wood. He didn't even have to think about not treading on them as he reached towards me.

"Here, Jules," he said.

I took his hand, and he pulled me into a friendly little foxtrot. He wasn't a bad lead, much better than Arthur or Jos. Each step glided into the next, as smooth as silk over glass. After a few unhurried turns and a funny twirl or two, he dipped me low.

"It's like Ma says—" He paused for a smile. "If you can't go over, go under."

When he swept me upright, we were on the roof.

Behind clouds and smog, the sun was setting over London.

"Cold!" I accused, caterpillaring my hands into my sleeves. I puffed my cheeks at him as the wind caught my hair.

"There's got to be a workman's door around here somewhere," said Simon as he searched, a shiver in his voice, but he was too long-suffering to complain. "Sorry. At least we're out. View's nice, innit?"

It was.

We crawled over the roof, feeling like goats on the side of a mountain as our fingers and toes steadily numbed into hooves, until we discovered an attic dormer was open. It led to one of the old servants' rooms, unoccupied for years, and empty save for a wrought-iron bed frame. I would have put my foot through the pane, but through magic or fortune or whatever you would call it, we were spared both the broken glass and Muv's inevitable sigh. We already had enough to explain.

"Jules," said Simon before I climbed in. I turned, blinking at him: well, go on. "Can we stay out here a moment longer?"

And what, I wondered, did he so enjoy about risking his beautiful young limbs to frostbite? The view again, perhaps—that incomparable view. It wasn't often he had the chance to feel on top of the world.

"Oh," I said, backing out of the window, "if you insist."

Orange smoke hung about the rooftops, sank into the alleys and eves. Everything was slightly hazy, slightly too small to be real. I was shivering, so Simon wrapped me in his arms. He was wonderfully solid and warm. I laid my head on his shoulder and told myself how easy it was not to cry.

EIGHT

THE BRACELET Uncle Vee gave me went to live at the bank with the other jewels. Muv said I could have it for the débutante parties in a year or two if I still wanted to participate. I did, of course, though *want* hardly came into it. I was always going to queue with Char and the rest of the girls, gaudy in our white trains and ostrich feathers, for our presentation at court; and then each of us would attend the others' coming out balls, a circuit of Victorian tedium. Grandad and Dorothy had already made themselves responsible for mine. After I was socially deemed an adult, that was when the fun would begin. I'd join the rest of the grown up young people, sparkling with champagne and melting over everybody's grandmothers' atrocious chaises longues.

So my thoughts ran as I practised my lunges in the nursery. According to Miss Talbot, my form was sloppy. I'd rushed past the fundamentals too quickly, which was all very well for a school whose principal aim was to promote graceful movement and healthy activity, but if I was to get any further in competition, I had to retrain my muscles properly.

Start slowly, Miss Talbot had told me. I leaned into the tension in my thighs, rocked through the shift in weight from back foot to front. As I increased the tempo of the exercise—step, step, lunge, and back—I envisioned myself grinding the routine into my bones. Step, step, lunge, and back. I must be fluid, I told myself, assertive. I was creating new instincts on which to rely during a bout.

I would have to marry someone or other eventually. Georgia was making the rounds now; though she wasn't much of an heiress, she was beautiful enough to nurture ambitions. For me the likeliest husband was dim old cheerful Arthur, unless the inevitable accident happened before we said our vows, in which case Joseph and I might concoct an arrangement. I would not say no, for both our sakes, and Marie and Adele would be thrilled to have me as their sister in more than spirit. I was already family.

If Muv had married Uncle Vee, I could have been Julia Vladimirovna.

I alternated positions, bringing my left foot to the front for another set of lunges without the foil. This was pure strength training; there was no sense in working my primary leg whilst leaving the other to atrophy. I let myself feel the ache.

The Koldunovs flocked to their father, Simon said. They adored Uncle Vee, and he courted their love. Their affections were a contest, his attention their reward.

My chest tightened when I thought about everything the Koldunov children hadn't been told about Uncle Vee. Surely they hadn't been told. They couldn't have known he was a lecher and worse. Unless they did, too well.

I picked up my foil. Another set.

How could Aunt Dahlia marry him if she knew the

sorts of things he'd done? Had she cared? Or was she too pleased she'd won the fairy prince? I'd always assumed she disliked Muv because she'd been Uncle Vee's first choice, never mind the other affairs, both Uncle Vee's and Aunt Dahlia's own. Self-declared libertines could be as hypocritical as anybody. Arthur was her child, no blood relation to Uncle Vee, but unlike Simon he was neither Jewish nor poor.

Step, step, lunge, and back.

If I'd been at school, I wouldn't have had to ponder any of this. (Step, step.) I wouldn't have to see Uncle Vee's charm from this new, ugly angle. I wouldn't have to reinterpret the times he'd complimented me, or given me a present, or hugged his children. (Lunge.) I wouldn't have to carry this knowledge like a boa constrictor lumping around with a dead mouse in its gut.

Digest already, I thought. Let me be lazy little Jules, nothing but bubbles in her brain. Take this sword out of my hand.

My palm was sweating in its glove.

The Koldunovs were supposed to be the happy family. They had the doting parents, the exquisite children, the lively household. There was space for me; there would always be a space for Alyechka's little girl. Only I no longer wanted to fit.

NINE

THE BELL rang, and the last round began. Simon had won the first round, and his opponent had claimed the second. Tired as they were, breathing heavily, the boys seemed more alert than ever. Sweat coated their bare chests and arms, those limber boxers' muscles. Simon didn't hesitate to show off his physical prowess, not here. When he danced in for a jab, I held my breath, and then gasped—yes!—when his glove connected with the other boy's jaw. I cheered from my place by the ring, my voice drowned in everyone else's. Behind me, Muv still clapped as though she were at the opera.

When the hollering subsided, she picked up where she had left off with Ruta. "It's not only Chamberlain; nobody in Cabinet enjoys meeting with me, but they convince themselves they're keeping me in check."

"So you've got famous enemies, same as me and everyone here, but they don't invite the likes of us for tea. Can't all be notorious lady magicians, can we?" She flicked Muv's pearl drop earring before she turned back to the match and said, even louder, "Do us a favour, love, and banish Disraeli's mouldering ghost."

"I'm afraid ghosts aren't my speciality; ask your son."

Another cheer arose; Simon's opponent finally maneuvered past his canny defences, landing a blow on my boy's cheek. His head snapped backward before he caught himself, and he blinked into the sort of fierce, jovial smile that in my experience signalled a fresh resolve to trounce the blighter opposite. About time, I thought. Too often he'd rather block hits than venture his own.

Ruta and I yelled our encouragement. Muv watched Simon until she was satisfied he'd not suffered an actual injury, and then continued: "He's a thoughtful student. Good-natured, perhaps to a fault, but I don't intend he should ever be forced to compromise his principles."

"Oh, you don't *intend*. It's the nature of the job, innit?"

"He needn't take up my position."

"Tell him a thousand times, and he'll still feel like he's got to. Magicians!" Ruta exhaled her mocking contempt. "My boy was going to be a rabbi."

"He still can be. I'm curious what you would think of that."

"'Cause I'm an atheist? Doesn't mean I'm not a Jew. You're a bad Catholic girl, you ought to know."

I hardly ever heard Muv laugh, but she and Ruta indulged in the chuckle of a private joke. So she'd found someone else, then, who'd actually listen to her go on about magic and ritual and the Church.

She had accepted Ruta's invitation—a challenge aimed at her and me, as Simon had no idea—to watch his next boxing club match. Ruta wasn't much taller than either Muv or me, so the three of us stood nearest the ring, close enough to see the sweat licking down Simon's curls. He was too occupied to notice us among the rest of the spectators.

We received some curious looks, but most people were content to ignore the lot of us, Ruta included; the few women present exchanged a few whispers on seeing her, nothing more. While her exploits did not make her especially beloved, Simon was very much the pride of his neighbourhood if the cheers were any indication. The crowd mainly consisted of young men and boys, speaking mostly English, though the older fellows sometimes launched into other languages. Russian I recognised, and Ruta told me the others were Polish and Yiddish.

I rather liked the crush, everybody united in their appreciation of athletic skill. Muv hid how dreadfully the noise overwhelmed her; she didn't want to seem like Lady So-and-so gone slumming at the common people's sport to demonstrate how interested and superior she was. We still were Lady So-and-sos, Muv and I, and Ruta was delighted not to let us forget it.

While seeming to pay attention to the match, which I was—good on you, Si, get him!—I kept listening to Ruta and Muv.

"I was in it to shock my parents. Smoking, drinking and the rest, staggering home at dawn. Sound familiar? Dragged you back to yours often enough, but we know whose fault that was. The times I took up with Vee were pure spite," added Ruta, "but then I only knew him after his brother died. Gloried in the infamy, didn't he?"

"He did, yes, though he has always genuinely appreciated art, for what that's worth." Not much, in Muv's opinion. "Those parties were his way of creating a world under his control, after the misery of the inquest and the amputation. His foot helped him to claim self-defence, though the papers concentrated upon the Koldunovs' tragedy rather than the other woman who died. She was my lady's maid. I counted every word they spared for her. It was better than reading what was written about me, which I've no doubt was equally shameful in quite another way."

"I'd tell you to read my paper instead if it weren't in Yiddish."

"If you send it to me, I'll learn."

The two of them had, for one particular minute, pitched their voices to burn certain daughterly ears. My blush was fierce. I didn't see why Muv could tell a stranger these things and not me, never mind that Ruta was no stranger, and never mind that I hadn't asked her. Not yet.

Their repartee sunk beneath the clamour brought on by another hit. Simon had thrown two punches: one to misdirect, and one to stagger the other boy, shoulder to toe.

As the wave of cheers receded, I heard Ruta saying, "You're no exception."

"I do what I can," said Muv, as impassioned as I'd ever heard her. "Were it in my power, we parasites would—"

Simon's opponent slammed him up with a cut to the jaw, and then whipped him down with a mean left hook. A classic move, and a clear win. As the referees made their call, I applauded for a match well-fought.

"—I meant it, both Millie and me keep other company. I'd like to see you dine somewhere without fifty different forks, try some honest fish and chips."

"I would be delighted, but only if Simon agrees. He may prefer these parts of his life continue to be kept separate."

"And you come to his boxing match without telling him?"

Muv sounded horribly smug. "I had my reasons."

Even though Simon had lost, he grinned as sweet as clover to the bees when he shook hands with his opponent. Water was brought, and towels. I couldn't hear what he was saying to the other boy, but Simon's look and laugh had a more significant edge. He seemed conscious of their being shirtless, yes, except he wasn't embarrassed; no, he was enjoying the tension. Was this lanky young man the fabled Max? Whoever he was, Simon must have known him well. Even when he was performing magic of another sort, his confidence was delightful. He was in his element, his charm at its brightest for the sake of a handsome boy.

When he'd finished drying off, he slung the towel about his neck and descended from the ring. "Ma!" he called, and with a wave he found her. "I'm getting a loser's pint with the lads, you can go home." Then he saw Muv and me. He stopped. His accent softened. "Oh. Hullo, Lady Aloysia, ma'am, I wasn't expecting—er. The honour?"

"If you're getting a pint, then, I'll come with," I said, to which Muv instantly replied, "You will not."

"I invited them," said Ruta. "No need to thank me."

"Thanks, Ma." Simon wasn't angry, just startled. He turned a smile on me. "Fancy seeing you here, Jules. How was I?"

"Acceptable, I suppose."

He lightly punched my arm, so I punched his. Then he put up his fists, so I slid into *en garde* as though I had my foil. We sparred for a moment or two before Simon began throwing subtle glances elsewhere. He was looking for his friends. I understood. Simon wasn't ready to introduce Miss Selwyn-Stirling to his East End comrades. He mightn't ever be ready. I didn't mind. I wasn't offended. Muv and I were starting to impose on his space, that was all, and I felt we ought to take our leave.

We had no reason to stay, except neither of us wanted to be alone with the other.

After he shook hands with Muv and accepted her compliments, I shooed Simon off to his friends. Ruta walked with Muv and me to the exit, where we collected our winter things, and they continued what appeared to be, astonishingly enough, a *mutual* flirtation. I wouldn't have thought Muv had it in her. Simon would be so very embarrassed. I mulled over funny ways to break the news, hopping from foot to foot as our parents moved from potential dinner plans to more of their old acquaintances, painters and photographers, suffragists and anarcho-syndicalists. Only my mother could dawdle over such dreary subjects as labour rights and public health.

Finally, each of them having fired one last parting shot, Muv and I left the building, an old hotel converted into a Jewish community athletics club. The plan was to walk the several streets to where the driver waited. Muv thought it'd be obtrusive and conspicuous for Grandad's Daimler to show up out front, even if there were any room for the hulking thing. At least the weather was no more awful than usual.

The streets weren't as quiet as they were in Mayfair. More children were about, more passers-by, men and women headed to and from the markets or their work. Well done, Muv, I was tempted to say; you have exposed your cloistered, indolent daughter to a broader spectrum of humanity. Instead I watched her give two-fingered taps to the corner of every third building. Once or twice or more upon a time, she must have left her blood. All that work. Muv never missed an opportunity to repeat her rituals, and the stares had long since ceased to trouble her.

I was surprised when she spoke first. "Did you enjoy the boxing match, Julia?"

Though I was by this point tired of the walking and the cold and the strange looks, my tone was light. "When has my enjoyment mattered to you?"

"More often than not, I should hope. I am your mother."

But she always had another agenda. "Well," I said, "I enjoyed it very much, seeing Simon at his sport. All those brawny, scantily-clad boys! What a corrupting influence you are. Speaking of, I do like Simon's mother. She has opinions, doesn't she? Like you."

"Ruta Wolf is a fascinating woman." Muv tapped a shop corner.

"What does the pattern mean?"

She fixed me with one of her inscrutable stares. "Are you truly interested in the answer, or are you once again postponing this conversation we are about to have?"

"You were doing it too." I fidgeted with the fringe on my scarf. I kicked at pebbles. I blew warmth on my mittened hands. And, because I had to be the one to do it, I gave in. "Do you really think we're parasites?"

"Yes," said Muv. "The aristocracy is outdated and unnecessary, both morally and civically unconscionable. Our way of life engenders cruelty and complacency. I am guilty of both, but as I told Ruta Wolf, I do what I can. When I was young, younger than you, Julia, I learned of certain injustices in this world. I had no choice but to experience them firsthand. Once I learned to be angry at the treatment of women within our own class, the rest of my anger followed as a matter of course."

"Logic," I said. "Right."

She didn't seem angry; she never did. She talked at her usual clip and strode at her usual pace. I had to trot to keep up.

"You were curious about one of my journals," Muv continued, tapping another building. "Miss Eileen Dempsey was employed as my companion and chaperone. She was the second person Nikolai killed, though her death was a more honest accident; he had certainly meant to hurt Liza, if not kill her outright."

I winced. "I'm sorry."

"For what? You had nothing to do with it."

Muv's feelings were never easy to read. I couldn't peer inside her head, see for myself the strings that kept her together, but no one knew her like I did. Even before she'd banished my father, the two of us were, well, not friends, but necessary allies. She was only this brittle when she couldn't figure out how else to be. She was anxious, perhaps, or—for once in her life—worried she had been too blunt with me.

"I mean, I'm sorry that happened," I said. "And if you're upset about it, I'm sorry I went through your journals."

The traffic around us thinned; Muv had led us onto a residential street lined with brown brick flats. Simon grew up, if not precisely here, then somewhere very like it, in a narrow flat brimming with Ruta's pamphlets and his stacks of books.

Muv went on with her tapping.

"I am not upset with you," she said. "I have been wondering whether I was right to wait until you came to me. Perhaps I was not, but I believe there is value in exploring certain things for one's self. I would have wanted to do the same."

"So—all right, I'm still sorry for what happened, then."

"For what Nikolai did," she corrected.

When we turned the corner, Grandad's London driver, Bill, stubbed out his cigarette on the wall he was leaning against and tipped his hat to Muv. I noticed people noticing him as he opened the door for us, but that distraction lasted only until we were seated within the Daimler's glass and steel. The partition separated us from Bill.

And there we were: Muv and me alone, together.

She touched my shoulder. She was delicate, at first, but then she gave it a squeeze. Her hands must have ached something awful from the cold. With her cheeks so pink and her hair tousled into its natural curl, she looked much younger. More like me.

The engine shuddered to life.

"I did love him," she said. Prince Nikolai or Uncle Vee? "I loved them all."

As the car pulled away, she folded her hands on her lap. I wished Simon were here to guess if she was enacting magic, which was foolish of me; the better question was if she ever stopped.

A minute passed before Muv spoke again. "The

attentions he paid me were cruel, I know that now. He treated his younger siblings no better. Vladimir may have been a collaborator, as well as a bully in his own right, but he was not exempt. When I confided in her, Liza thought we three should band together and tell our parents. You've met your grandfather. It wouldn't have done much good."

But their word should have counted for something. Right?

"He did not mean to kill her when he pushed her down the stairs. A broken arm would have sufficed." She stared out the window. "Nothing came of the inquest— as you might imagine, Nikolai was very convincing, not least because his grief was real—but Vladimir and I had learned our lesson. Our silence was guaranteed."

Of course Muv had known what I'd been about to ask. It was almost unthinkable that my mother, my crisp, cutting mother, should have been denied her voice. At present it was level and clear, but it lacked the intensity with which she discussed magic with Simon, or politics with Ruta. I'd never heard a lecture so consciously blank.

"I cannot remember what the initial fight was about. After Liza's death, they were always fighting over one thing or another. Eileen and I had the misfortune to be present for this one; my family often stayed at the Koldunovs' house. Trust Vladimir to reclaim that particular room as his study."

It was where Simon and I held our séance.

"The pistol belonged to Nikolai," she said. "The first shot he fired was intended to be a warning, to scare Vladimir. The second eventually killed Eileen, who attempted to interfere. The third destroyed Vladimir's left foot. He then wrested away the gun and shot Nikolai, twice, with what I can only call astonishing accuracy." She made a point of tugging at her glove. "I must have known what I was doing. Seventeen is old enough to be culpable."

A patterned rug, smoke, silence—and I experienced a sudden, deep emptiness, as though my skull were a decorative egg blown hollow of its brains. I shivered. I had a capable imagination, but with Muv there was always a question of whose thoughts belonged to whom.

"I was of little use as a witness. After the inquest, and once Vladimir's injury had sufficiently healed, their parents retired to the country. Vladimir established his notorious social circle, of which I more or less willingly became a part. I was lonely, and Nikolai and Eileen were dead. I married myself into an escape, of sorts, but when your father and I returned to London—" Her voice tightened. "Vladimir had children. And then I had you. There's an adage about keeping your enemies close, isn't there? Few indeed have this sort of power. I believe I must use mine."

Of course she did.

"While she lived," Muv said, "Eileen protected me. Out of necessity, she curtailed my freedom; I hope I have improved upon her model by giving you yours."

My breath seemed far too loud. It clouded the pane and poured back, warm and damp, upon my cheek.

"Muv," I said, turning to her.

"Yes?" She blinked at me.

I was unsure how to continue. "Can I thank you?"

"I don't need thanks, but you may, if you like."

"Thank you, then."

After several moments, Muv laid her hand on my wrist, briefly, and then withdrew. "My bright girl. Not much escapes your notice."

Compliments from her were rare, and yet—they were deeply considered. Never thoughtless, always true. I wished I had something more special for her than a bewildered shrug.

"What about the other Koldunovs?" She wasn't going to answer until I came up with a more specific question.

"Marie and Adele and everyone, do they know?" After daring another glance at Muv, I crossed my arms and waited, watching the brick and smoke of the East End give way to the grey, familiar pomp of the West.

Finally, she spoke. "You're wondering, then, whether you are obligated to warn your friends about their father, lest he attempt to do them harm."

She would bring moral obligation into it.

"First, I assure you—indeed, I *assure* you—that Vladimir will never be alone with any member of his staff, any of his children's young friends, or any of his children; in short, anyone who is not a willing and equal adult. I wish I could think better of him, especially with respect to his own family, but my trust is better placed elsewhere.

"Second," she went on, "it is your choice whether or not to share what you have learned with the Koldunov children. For my part, I have left that decision to their mother. Dahlia is aware they will come to no harm. Beyond that, she prefers I not interfere. I respect her reasoning, even if I disagree. Her children are not mine to raise. Mind you—if any of them were to ask me what happened between their father, his family, and myself, I would tell them the truth. As I am telling you."

I was nodding along, still looking anywhere but at my mother. I wasn't near tears. I wasn't flushed or flustered. I wasn't feeling much of anything; it was as though my heart was storing up all the emotions for later, to let loose at the most inconvenient time possible. More than anything I just wanted this conversation to be done, or better yet for it to have *been* done, an hour or a day or a whole week past.

At least my curiosity was satisfied. At least Muv could have her say.

She'd gone quiet by then, but she hadn't withdrawn. Was I supposed to interject? Or was she not finished? If I were silent any longer, I'd have to start performing the correct reaction, whatever that meant, right there in front of my all-seeing mother, and that would be too much for either of us to bear.

So I affected a sulk and said, "Did you bring me to Simon's boxing match to get me somewhere I couldn't run off?"

"Partially," Muv admitted. "I thought you might like to see it. I know you're contemplating an athletic career."

"I am?" I paused. "You did?"

"Julia, please." She straightened her hat and gloves, small mannerisms by which she composed herself into herself again; it was the only indication of how grateful she was we'd returned to familiar ground. "You never talked about school unless you could bring up the fencing club. You asked for your own foil and gloves for your thirteenth birthday, and this winter your mood did not improve until you began lessons with Miss Talbot. Since then, I've not passed a single day without hearing you thump about upstairs. But do go on, tell me you haven't a vested interest."

"Oh, *Muv*," I groaned.

"Miss Talbot is impressed. She says if you train diligently enough, you might try for the next Olympic Games."

"The Olympics, me? I couldn't."

"You could, in fact, but you are not obligated," Muv said. "I am simply informing you of your options."

It was a peculiar relief Muv could still be prim and sanctimonious after all that, even when she was trying to encourage me. "I thought you wanted me otherwise occupied whilst you and Simon vexed divine powers we frail mortals wot not of. I didn't realise this was a—a conspiracy to teach me the importance of hard work and practice."

She offered me a cryptic smile. "And no magic was necessary."

"Muv!"

TEN

THE ROOM whose dormer had been so precipitously open for Simon and I, the one nearest the nursery, must have belonged to Eileen. I was no magician; I was only quick about drawing the obvious connections. I didn't blame Dolly and Beth for cleaning the old maids' quarters less often; there was hardly anything on which dust might land, only bare wooden floors and an iron bed frame, as we'd seen before, without its mattress. The squares where pictures once hung were almost as faded as the rest of the wallpaper.

I set my candle on the floor. The afternoon sun, weak and wintry though it was, proved quite enough to illuminate such a small room. The candle burned for reasons I'd decided were mysterious and symbolic, magic only in the sense that anything could be magic, even my vague notions of respect.

After several minutes, as promised, Simon came in and sat beside me, crossing his legs so he could lean his elbows on his knees.

"Thanks," I said. "You needn't summon any ghosts, I promise. I only want them to know I know they're here, if they are. Is that strange?"

"Even if it were, would you care?"

"Tremendously."

Our silence lasted only a short while before I summoned up my courage and filled it. Muv had expected I'd confide in Simon, and I did want to. I knew I ought to. He was my friend.

The candle's flame shivered as I told him how Liza and Eileen died, how Muv's magic helped to kill Prince Nikolai. When I explained her spell on Uncle Vee, Simon searched my face so he could properly reflect what I might be feeling. Horror, admiration, gratitude? Everything? Nothing? I pressed my lips together. Letting him hug me was easier than trying to sort out words I didn't have.

"Can he tell what she's doing?" Simon asked, finally lifting his head from my shoulder. "Has he got any idea?"

"He may. Or not." I shrugged. "They've a large family. None of them are left much to themselves, not even Lizzie."

"I wonder how much his knowing matters, if it's her revenge."

"Oh, I'm certain it is, at least a little," I said.

"What else? Besides ensuring he won't hurt anyone else, I mean. She still sees him—repetition is how her magic…" He trailed off. "It can't be pleasant for her."

"Penance," I suggested, and the weight of truth settled into my bones. "It's not pleasant because it's not supposed to be."

Simon exhaled. "I wish we hadn't been right. Doesn't seem fair, does it? Prince Vladimir gets to go on with his life, not as he did, but there's such a thing as public scorn. People are ostracised for less. Or put in jail." His fingers curled into the fabric of his trousers, as though he'd stopped himself from wringing his hands.

Perhaps he wasn't only thinking of his mother. "Are you going to tell the others? Marie and Adele?"

"I could," I said slowly. But— "They adore their father. If they believed me, it would break their hearts." If they didn't, it would break mine.

In the stillness of the room, the candle went out. We looked at it, at the smoke curling upward, and then at each other.

"What are we supposed to do?"

"I don't know, Jules," he said. "The best we can?"

ELEVEN

Miss Talbot's rigorous new training schedule was hardly my least favourite present. That honour belonged to the morocco-bound, gilt-tooled set of Gibbon's *Decline and Fall of the Roman Empire* my father saw fit to send his only child on the occasion of her seventeenth birthday.

"You do like unearthing ancient history," Muv airily supposed, and I was forced to admit she had a sense of humour.

The detective novels were a nice addition to what we both understood was her true present: if I were serious about a fencing career, I needn't complete a final year at another school. I could stay home and pester Simon for as long as I liked.

His gift was a new deck of cards. "Unmarked," he said, adding a pointed look.

I cheated nonetheless when we tried them out for the first time, on our picnic at the Kensington Gardens. Taking advantage of the unusual late March warmth, like everybody else in London, we held my birthday party out of doors. Muv and Simon and I had our blanket, and the Koldunovs poured across three of their own.

I'd been thoroughly fêted, lavished with praise and loved upon. Bouquets of white and yellow rosebuds rested beside plates of egg-and-watercress sandwiches, rounds of cheese, bunches of fat grapes, bowls as pellucid and dainty as the caviar within. No picnic could be more perfect. Yet I couldn't shake off, and by rights probably hadn't ought to, the creeping premonition this delightful family outing with the Koldunovs was to be the last.

There would be other outings, surely. Even here, with the sun bearing down on the broad, glittering pond, on trees just barely touched with green, things weren't so crystalline as I wished they could be, one last time.

We were entering the idle portion of the afternoon, in which nobody wanted to do anything but lay about like enormous cats. Georgia was reading Tolstoy beneath the shade of her wide-brimmed hat; Joseph, home for Easter week but still in uniform, and not to be outdone by his elder sister, was pretending he could read Latin without translating it first. Every so often, Arthur would offer Marie and Adele and me sips of whisky from the flask Aunt Dahlia carefully declined to notice—as she declined to notice everything else she'd rather not address.

Everyone but me, it seemed, was ignoring Muv and Uncle Vee.

The two of them stood apart from the rest of us, Uncle Vee elegant in his linen scarf and boater hat, leaning on his cane, and Muv poised in a suit of violet-grey. He murmured to her, laid a knuckle on her chin; she turned away. He cajoled, slightly louder, in Russian-flavoured French, and circled his hand around her wrist.

She looked up at him with such calm, pitying disgust, it was a wonder he didn't kneel in her web and draw the gossamer threads about his own guilty neck.

"Volodya," she said.

He released her and, as he strode away, swept a sardonic bow.

I was pretty certain what their argument was about. When we'd arrived at the park, Uncle Vee came towards me for a peck on the cheek, and I'd presented him with a handshake instead.

"Ah, yes," he'd said, trying to draw me into the joke, "our Yulechka is seventeen now, much too old and proud for a kiss from her Uncle Vee."

"An ancient crone preserved in a bog and all that," I heard myself say, and before Adele dragged me away to perform dramatic readings of the latest *Tatler*, I saw him glare at Muv.

She stood alone now, at the edge of the pond. A gust of wind toyed with her hair.

When I'd finished retrieving the last of my new playing cards from where they'd blown across the lawn, Marie and Adele gestured for me to join them on their blanket. I hesitated. Which way was Uncle Vee headed? Did it matter? Waving at the girls, and indicating the cards with which I exaggeratedly fanned myself, I sat beside Simon for another round. Lizzie, dreadful child, was welcome to observe.

Uncle Vee approached us. I made a show of examining my hand.

"I see my youngest has attached herself to you," he said to Simon. Indeed, Lizzie's hands were clamped about his arm.

"I don't know why, sir," said Simon. He picked up a stray flower from one of my bouquets, a furled white rose; the moment his breath crossed its petals, it bloomed.

Lizzie unglued herself from Simon to grab the rose, and then started pulling off its petals in great, sticky handfuls. Uncle Vee ruffled her curls. "Well," he said, "so long as you don't turn this one into a pot of roses, there's no harm in it. Got the magic sorted, have you?"

Simon met his gaze, unblinking. "I've learned a thing or two, yes."

"Excellent, excellent. There's some power in our blood."

"Funny, that. Lady Aloysia told me magic doesn't work that way."

"Is that so?" Uncle Vee's smile became so very kind as his beautiful blue eyes flashed. "I'm glad I introduced you to Alya. Hell of a woman, isn't she?"

"She's a great magician, sir."

"So is Simon," I added, having used the distraction to slide my nine of spades into the stock pile and withdraw an ace. "Your turn."

"Indeed." With one last elegant bow, Uncle Vee took Lizzie's hand—"Let's leave the nice young people to their game, shall we?"—and returned to the glow of his children's attention.

"Papa," Adele pouted, "Jos said I had a *risu inepto*, what does it mean?"

"A silly laugh, because you do," Jos huffed.

"Papa, look, Gee's in the paper—"

"Masha, dearest, it's nothing."

"*The enchanting Miss Georgia Koldunova*," Marie began, and she recited the rest of the article louder and louder over her siblings' ongoing chatter. No family could be more pleasantly annoyed with each other as they basked. The sunlight adored them, the whole set; they shone like precious gems.

I squeezed Simon's hand. He squeezed mine back.

"I've made a decision," he said. "I *am* looking forward to having you at our seder."

"As you should, but Muv will ask all sorts of questions," I warned.

"She's wise, you're wicked, the other two I don't know—it's a joke, Jules, I'll explain it tomorrow."

"The wise son, the wicked son, the simple son, and the son who doesn't know how to ask," Muv said, smoothing her skirt as she resumed her place on the blanket beside Simon. "Is that right? I've been apprising myself of Passover custom; I shouldn't like to offend. Thank you for inviting us, by the way."

Cheerfully, he replied, "I probably won't regret it."

We made a picturesque trio, Muv and Simon and I, two clever ladies and our handsome young escort. Or: England's two most accomplished magicians and their favourite clown. Two friends whose guardian and guide wouldn't let us shoulder the weight of anyone else's mistakes.

Which was quite all right, I thought, as I lay on my back and looked up to the wide, blue sky. We'd simply have to make more mistakes of our own.

ACKNOWLEDGEMENTS

THANK YOU to Annie Metcalf, Dena Shapiro, Lara Mirante, Meagan Kane, and Sara Pace, who always give us inspiration. And thank you to Katharine Anderson and Lulav Arnow for talking us through the first draft.

For keen feedback, encouragement, and discussion, our thanks to Alison Rumfitt, Chana Perlman, Elyse Martin, Emma Mieko Candon, Julia August, Lara Sichi, Marissa Lingen, and Sacha Lamb.

And all our love to Anna Bergslien, Ann Sparks (z"l), Wade and Beth Bergslien, Sean Weaver and Corinne Weaver Reimann, Brogan Farren and Scott Weaver, and Dave and Karen Campbell.